A Dark, Handsome Stranger

You wander over to a dock and plop down on the steps of a building, soaking in the excitement, listening to the music of the Italian language. Twenty yards away, about fifteen artists are standing at their easels painting. One of the painters is not much older than you; he has dark, wavy hair and prominent cheekbones. He is staring right at you.

You nervously turn in the other direction, suddenly conscious of the way you are sitting. You cross your legs and fold your arms in your lap. A few minutes later, you quickly glance in the painter's direction and jerk your head back immediately. Not only is this person still staring at you, but now he is walking directly toward you.

What do I do? you frantically think. *He's getting closer. He's smiling at me.*

If you get up quickly and walk away, turn to page 42.

If you stay seated, turn to page 92.

FOLLOW YOUR HEART ROMANCES for you to enjoy

#1 SUMMER IN THE SUN
 by Jan Gelman

#2 BOYS! BOYS! BOYS!
 by Jan Gelman

#3 A STAGE SET FOR LOVE
 by Caroline Cooney

#4 SUN, SEA AND BOYS
 by Caroline Cooney

#5 FARAWAY LOVES
 by Jan Gelman

#6 TAKE A CHANCE ON LOVE
 by Jan Gelman

#7 RACING TO LOVE
 by Caroline Cooney

#8 LOTS OF BOYS
 by Jan Gelman

#9 SUNTANNED DAYS
 by Caroline Cooney

Available from ARCHWAY paperbacks

Most Archway Paperbacks are available at special quantity discounts for bulk purchases for sales promotions, premiums or fund raising. Special books or book excerpts can also be created to fit specific needs.

For details write the office of the Vice President of Special Markets, Pocket Books, 1230 Avenue of the Americas, New York, New York 10020.

#8 *A Multiple Choice Romance* — FOLLOW YOUR HEART

LOTS OF BOYS!

JAN GELMAN

AN ARCHWAY PAPERBACK
Published by POCKET BOOKS • NEW YORK

AN ARCHWAY PAPERBACK *Original*

An Archway Paperback published by
POCKET BOOKS, a division of Simon & Schuster, Inc.
1230 Avenue of the Americas, New York, N.Y. 10020

Copyright © 1985 by S & R Gelman Associates, Inc. and
Jan Gelman
Cover photograph copyright © 1985 Rich Vogel

All rights reserved, including the right to reproduce
this book or portions thereof in any form whatsoever.
For information address Pocket Books, 1230 Avenue
of the Americas, New York, N.Y. 10020

ISBN: 0-671-53158-1

First Archway Paperback printing April, 1985

10 9 8 7 6 5 4 3

AN ARCHWAY PAPERBACK and colophon are
registered trademarks of Simon & Schuster, Inc.

FOLLOW YOUR HEART is a trademark
of Simon & Schuster, Inc.

Printed in the U.S.A.

IL 5+

For Jean-Louis, Laura, Patrizia, Marzio, Steve, Shirley, the Tchekovs, and all the other wonderful people who made my travels in Europe so memorable.

And a special thanks to my Italian professor, Stefano Hughes.

Read This First!

Lots of Boys! is not an ordinary romance book. It will not make sense if you try to read the pages consecutively. Instead, read until you come to a choice. Then follow your choice to the page indicated. Again, read until you come to a choice; then follow the instructions.

When you reach an ending, the book is not over. Just go back to the beginning and make different choices. You can lose—but only temporarily. There is always another chance.

So follow your heart, read your way to romance, and have a good time.

1

"What do you mean you want *me* to decide?" you say. "You're the one who's looking for a job."

You and your mother are sitting on the floor, surrounded by mounds of brochures.

"I know. I know. But both jobs are great, and I can't make up my mind. Venice, Italy, is an incredible place for an art historian to work; and you know how much I love burying myself in museums. I know I'd have a wonderful time. But it's only a temporary job. When my year is up, I'd have to start all over again searching for a permanent teaching position at an American university . . . and who knows where we'd end up.

"If I took the job in Crystal, Colorado, we'd finally be settled. You could make friends and spend your last two years of high school in one place. I know it hasn't been easy for you, moving around so much. And there's a part of me, too, that really

(continued on page 2)

would like to be settled. Besides, this is your life, too. Really, you'll be doing me a favor if you make the decision."

You have been hearing about nothing else for the last two weeks, but it's always been your mother's problem. Suddenly, it's yours.

Venice, Italy. You can picture yourself in the moonlight being serenaded by a gorgeous Italian man as he maneuvers his gondola through the narrow canals. You, of course, are snuggled next to the boy of your dreams while he whispers beautiful Italian words in your ear. There's something very exciting about the unknown.

But there's also the fear. Just thinking about being in a foreign country scares you. You don't even speak the language. How could you ever make friends? Even with all the moving around you've done, at least you have been able to speak the language. Besides, Colorado sounds kind of nice: the mountains, the snow, the rivers, and all the outdoor sports like water-skiing, mountain climbing, hiking, snow skiing—to say nothing of all the college guys at the university.

If you choose to go to Venice for a year, go to page 3.

If you choose to move to Colorado, turn to page 7.

LOTS OF BOYS! 3

"Wake up," your mother says as you groggily open your eyes. We're almost there!"

You squint to block out the bright sun that is streaming into the window of the train. When your eyes have adjusted, you stare out at a wide canal that is lined with buildings. There is no sidewalk in front of the buildings, just a narrow step, and then the water.

The train jolts to a stop. You pull your suitcase from the rack above your head and follow your mother through the narrow aisle and onto the platform. There are masses of people rushing by you, hugging, laughing, yelling in a language you don't understand. You are frightened and excited at the same time.

Suddenly you feel a hand on your suitcase. A man in a brown suit is shoving a photograph of a building in front of your face.

"Hotel? Nice hotel?" he says.

"No, thanks," you say, taking control of your suitcase and moving away from him.

You are shaken by the experience. You look around for your mother, but you don't see her. All you can see is the crowd, and all you can hear are incomprehensible sounds. You don't even notice the tall, slightly heavy man with a gray beard who is holding a sign with your mother's name on it. Your mother rushes over and greets him. She calls to you, and you hurry over.

(continued on page 4)

"Hello. Welcome to Venice," he says loudly in an Italian accent. "I am Antonio Bandonelli, the director of your museum project. We have talked by mail. I will take you to your home." He takes your suitcases.

You follow him onto a dock and wait with a crowd of other people for a boat. You have seen millions of pictures of Venice, with its canals and boats, but somehow you never realized until now that the canals are like streets. Instead of buses or cars, people get around by boat! The canal is filled with boat traffic.

"Ah, my beautiful women, you will love Venice. It is the most wonderful place in the world," says Mr. Bandonelli.

You already agree as you pass by old castles and arched buildings with small boats docked in front of them. You pass under a bridge, and a long, thin boat with pointed ends enters from the other side. A man is standing at the rear of the boat, paddling.

"A gondola!" you shout. It's just as you had always pictured.

"Ah, yes, my dear," says Mr. Bandonelli. "And this is only one little part of the romance of Venice."

The bus-boat you are riding on pulls up to a dock, and you and your mother follow Mr. Bandonelli along the pier. Gondolas are lined up in the water like parked cars.

(continued on page 5)

LOTS OF BOYS!

"Now, we will go to your home," says Mr. Bandonelli as he winds in and out of narrow, car-less streets and alleys crowded with people. You are convinced that you will never be able to find your way around in this maze of streets and canals.

You pass by open restaurants filled with people and displays of seafood. You look into the windows of leather shops and grocery and dress stores.

"Americana, Americana," calls a man in front of one of the restaurants. "Eat here. Good food."

How does he know I'm American? you wonder. You smile at him and move on. After about ten minutes of walking, Mr. Bandonelli stops at an old, gray apartment building. You follow him up two flights of a dimly lit staircase.

"This is your new home!" he announces as he flings open a door.

The apartment is dark. There is a small living room, a kitchen, and a bedroom with two beds. In the bathroom, there is a tank hanging over the toilet.

"You know to pull the chain when you are finished?" says Mr. Bandonelli.

You have never seen a toilet like that before, but you nod your head.

"You must be very tired," Mr. Bandonelli says. "But I will offer you some choices." He looks at you and explains that the international school you

(continued on page 6)

will be attending has a weekly meeting for its foreign students. The meeting is scheduled for tonight, and he will bring you there if you choose to go.

"But," he continues, "if you want to wait and go to the meeting next week, my wife and I would very much like you both to come to our home for dinner tonight. She is a very good cook, and we would like to welcome you to Italy with a special dinner.

If you go to dinner, turn to page 11.

If you go to the meeting, turn to page 13.

LOTS OF BOYS!

You stare out your window. The view from your room is like something out of a travel magazine. Craggy mountains pierce the blue sky in all directions. White, fluffy clouds float overhead. Lush green trees dot the landscape. Colorado is the most beautiful place you have ever seen.

So why have I spent the last three days in tears? you wonder.

The answer is easy. You have been in Colorado for two weeks and the only person who has talked to you is your mother. Not a girl. Not a guy. Not even a little kid!

You and your mom have rented a wonderful A-frame house tucked into the side of a mountain; but there's not a neighbor in sight! The house is not far from the college campus, where there are a lot of students around—but what do they want with a junior in high school?

When you go into the village, you see kids your age, but they all have their own groups, and you are not a part of them. You are feeling lonely and sad and on the verge of tears all day long; and you are trying to hide it from your mother, which makes it even harder.

You have finally gotten to the point where you are either going to crawl under the covers and go to sleep for the rest of the summer, or you are going to get a job.

You throw on a pair of jeans and walk toward campus. You walk down a tree-lined path onto the

(continued on page 8)

college campus. A small bridge crosses a brook, and you sit for a minute on the railing. Then you move on, past the modern gymnasium with its glass-enclosed swimming pool.

As you walk past the college bookstore, you see a sign in the window: HELP WANTED.

Well, you think. *That's the reason for this trip. Get up the courage and do it!*

You walk in the door. The store is filled with students.

Summer session is about to begin, you think. *They must be getting ready for their classes.*

"Excuse me," you say to a girl at a cash register. "Where would I find the manager?"

She points to an office in the back of the store, and you walk toward it. Every step is an effort. You have never done anything like this before. You just turned sixteen, and the only job you've ever had is babysitting.

"Excuse me," you say to the woman in the office. "Are you the manager?"

"Yes," she answers.

"I would like to apply for the job," you say.

"Please come in," she says. "Take a seat."

You are shaking as you sit there.

"What year are you in?" she asks.

"Oh," you say. "I'm a junior in high school."

"High school?" she says with a condescending

(continued on page 9)

smile. "I'm sorry, but this job is only open to students at the college."

"Oh, I'm sorry," you say. "I didn't know."

"Quite all right," she says and goes back to her work.

You are feeling hurt and rejected as you walk quickly across the rest of the campus and into town. *That's it for today,* you think. *I'll just wander.*

You are window-shopping when you pass the Soup and Salad Days restaurant. There is a sign in the front window: WAITRESS WANTED.

By now you have calmed down. *Why not?* you think.

You walk inside. A woman in her mid-thirties walks over to you. You explain that you would like to apply for the job.

"Good," she says. "I had two people quit on me today." She asks you a few questions and offers you the job. "There's only one thing," she says. "I really need you tonight from six to ten. Can you do it?"

"No problem," you tell the woman, who introduced herself as Maggie. "I'll be back at six and ready to work."

Maggie hands you a pair of blue denim painter's pants. "Don't worry about the fit, they're supposed to be baggy. It's your responsibility to keep these clean. And we all wear white, short-sleeved shirts. Welcome aboard." She shakes your hand.

(continued on page 10)

You bounce back home, smiling for the first time in weeks.

"Mom, guess what?"

"From the way you've been acting lately, I'm afraid to guess," she says.

"No, this is good news. I got a job as a waitress and I start tonight."

"That's wonderful! Congratulations."

"The woman didn't even care that I've never waitressed before. She asked me if I was coordinated and I said yes. I think she was desperate!"

"Well, so what?" says your mother. "You've got a job! The rest is her problem."

You are showered and about to get dressed when you realize that neither you nor your mother has a short-sleeved white shirt. You glance at your watch. There is no way you can buy a shirt and still show up on time.

If you wear a pink, short-sleeved shirt and show up on time, turn to page 21.

If you shop for a white shirt and risk being late, turn to page 38.

LOTS OF BOYS!

Your mother looks at you for an answer. You are definitely not ready to meet a gang of kids yet.

"That is so nice of you and your wife to invite us," you say. "I would love to come for dinner." You are pleased to have your first meal with an Italian family.

"I hope you will be very hungry," says Mr. Bandonelli as he goes out the door. "I will come to get you at eight o'clock. *Ciao.*"

As Mr. Bandonelli closes the door, your mother collapses on the couch. "I'm exhausted!" she announces. "I'm going to take a nap."

You are much too overwhelmed by everything to think about sleeping. You flop into an armchair for a few minutes and think about whether or not you have the nerve to face this foreign world alone.

All right, you finally decide, *I'll just go for a short walk.*

You write down your address and phone number and put the paper in your pocket.

You walk through the narrow streets, along the canals, over the bridges. Venice is like a storybook come to life. Gondolas, ornate homes, sculpted bridges, laughter. There are children playing kickball, women hanging out clothes, churches that must have taken hundreds of years to build, bakeries, butchers, and, in the central square, thousands of pigeons flying, standing, eating, and getting their pictures taken by tourists.

You wander over to a dock and plop down on the

(continued on page 12)

steps of a building, soaking in the excitement, listening to the music of the Italian language. Twenty yards away, about fifteen artists are standing at their easels, painting. One of the painters is not much older than you; he has dark, wavy hair and prominent cheek bones. He is staring right at you.

You nervously turn in the other direction, suddenly conscious of the way you are sitting. You cross your legs and fold your arms in your lap. A few minutes later, you glance quickly in the painter's direction and jerk your head back immediately. Not only is this person still staring at you, but now he is walking directly toward you.

What do I do? you frantically think. *He's getting closer. He's smiling at me.*

If you get up quickly and walk away, turn to page 42.

If you stay seated, turn to page 92.

LOTS OF BOYS!   **13**

There are about forty kids your age at the meeting, and they speak French, Italian, German, and English. You are overwhelmed by the whole scene. Quietly, without talking to anyone, you take a seat in the back. You feel totally left out. The best part of the evening is when an American girl drops a whole tray of sodas and soaks four people, who exclaim in four different languages.

The next day you are angry. You know you should have made an effort to introduce yourself, to become a part of the group. Instead, you just sat there as though you didn't care. You are thinking about this as you wander through the streets and alleys. You are not focusing on where you are going.

When you look around, you find yourself in San Marco Square. You are staring up at a massive church with arched entrances when suddenly someone crashes into you and knocks you down. A blond girl with wild and curly hair is sitting on your leg.

The girl turns around and you discover that it is the clumsy American from last night.

"My flash, my batteries! Oh, brother," she screams.

Batteries are rolling all over the ground. The girl turns to you.

"I'm so sorry," she blurts out. "I mean, *mi dispiace!* I'm such a klutz! I mean, *sono* . . . oh, forget it!"

"It's all right," you say, giggling.

(continued on page 14)

"Oh, you speak English! I'm so glad. I forget Italian at times like this."

You lean over and pick up a battery. "Weren't you at the meeting last night?"

"Yes," she says. "I'm Duckie."

You introduce yourself and you both struggle to your feet.

"Hey, I'm on my way to the islands for the day. How about joining me?"

"Sure," you say. "Sounds great."

As the two of you walk toward the dock, three Italian men walk by you and stop.

"Ciao, belle ragazze. Americane?"

Duckie pokes you and smiles. "In case you just arrived, that means, Hi, beautiful girls. Are you American?" She turns to the men. "No," she answers. *"Non siamo Americane."*

"Di dove siete?" one man asks. Where are you from?

"Siamo di Jugoslavia," she giggles.

"Dove andate?" the man asks.

"He wants to know where we are going," she translates.

If you tell them that you are going to the islands, turn to page 79.

If you tell them you are going to meet your mothers, turn to page 16.

LOTS OF BOYS! 15

The "No way" wins. *No guts,* you tell yourself.

"I can't do it, Russell. I want to, but I can't."

"At least try," he says.

"Please. . . ." you say, plaintively.

"Well," he says. "I'm not going to force you." And he swings himself down to your level.

The two of you walk slowly back. He helps you down the rough spots and keeps checking to be sure you are all right, but the enthusiasm has gone out of him.

You picnic halfway down on a grassy slope, but you say very little to each other. The playful mood has disappeared.

"You know," Russell says as you get into the car, "if you only do what you've always been doing, you'll never discover anything new."

You know he is disappointed in you. But not nearly as much as you are in yourself.

The End

Duckie tells the guys that you are going to meet your mothers. She then links arms with you, pulling you away from the men. They follow you.

"Arrivederci! Goodbye," Duckie says harshly to the men, trying to get rid of them.

The men move off in another direction. *"Ciao!"* they call as they give up on you.

Duckie turns to you. "You have to be aggressive and blunt with these men. They love American girls and won't leave you alone. Unless you want to talk to them, get out of it fast. Sometimes if you walk with your arms linked, they won't bother you as much. All the Italians walk that way. Oh, and Italian men love blondes. I'm thinking of dyeing my hair just so I can walk down the street!"

You both laugh. Duckie is funny, and it's nice to be with someone who speaks Italian.

"Come on!" she yells, looking at her watch. "We've got to hurry. The boat for Burano is leaving in ten minutes."

The two of you run onto the boat and plant yourselves on the deck in two seats facing the sun.

As you near Burano, you observe the small seaside houses, the old boats, and the broken-down docks partially submerged in the water.

When the boat stops, you follow the flow of people through the small alleys of a fishing village, weaving around hanging sheets and shirts and towels. The smell of cheese, bacon, seafood, and spices

(continued on page 17)

LOTS OF BOYS!

pour out of kitchen windows. You can hear the clanking of pots and pans.

Soon your tiny street merges into a wide-open street, also car-less, and scattered with restaurants, shops, and markets.

"Ladies, beautiful American ladies," calls a man in a white tuxedo. "Come here! Come have a cold drink. I love beautiful girls in my restaurant."

He is a small man in his forties with a dark beard and a sparkle in his eyes. "Your beauty will make my food taste better. Please come in. I welcome you. I would like the pleasure to buy you a Coke."

You and Duckie look at each other. You look at the smiling man. You look back at each other.

"Why not?" you say.

"Yeah, right," says Duckie. "It's not as though we have a lot of appointments."

He escorts you to a table. You and Duckie are the only customers in the restaurant. Two waiters rush over to you; two young men come out of the kitchen and stand at your table, and an elderly man comes in the front door and joins the crowd staring at you. No one says a word.

"Do you get the feeling we're the main attraction in this circus?" asks Duckie.

"Maybe we should do a dance," you say.

"Or juggle," says Duckie.

"My name is Gianmarco Tagliapietra," the man in

(continued on page 18)

the tuxedo tells you as he hands you each a Coke and pulls up a chair.

Just then a group of about fifteen Italians walks through the door. They are all carrying cameras, tripods, lenses, and flashes. Giovanni jumps up to greet them.

"Ciao, Fulvio," he says to an older man who is the first to enter the room. The man appears to be leading a group of young people who are not much older than you.

Giovanni leads the group to a huge table at the other end of the room. He turns to you and calls out, "This man is Fulvio Rossino, the greatest photographer in Italy. Fulvio, come and meet these beautiful Americans," he says in English . . .

Fulvio walks with him to your table and the two men sit down. A young man also walks over and stands next to your table. He is just about your age and has dark, curly hair that falls softly around his tanned face and his sparkling green eyes. He is wearing a bright orange shirt and Mickey Mouse sunglasses. He lifts up his glasses and stares at you. You look up and he smiles. You quickly look away.

This guy is kind of strange, you think, trying not to laugh.

The owner of the restaurant explains that Rossino teaches photography by traveling with his students. They always come to his restaurant to eat when they are on Burano.

(continued on page 19)

LOTS OF BOYS!

You look up. The young man is still staring at you. He keeps putting his glasses on, then lifting them up and winking at you. You look nervously around to see if anyone else has noticed.

"It is time to eat," says the owner, walking toward the kitchen.

The young man walks backward to his table, still looking at you. He bumps into a chair and knocks it over. You laugh.

Rossino gets up. "You must eat *risotto di pesce*," he says. *"Molto buono!"* He kisses the tips of his fingers and throws the kiss into the air.

How Italian! you think. *Just like in the movies.* Rossino returns to his table.

As soon as Rossino leaves, the young man comes back to your table. He reaches out and takes your hand and kisses the back of it.

"You are more beautiful when you smile. I am Dario," he says in a soft, deep voice.

Duckie kicks your leg under the table, and you both introduce yourselves.

Dario smiles. "I am happy to know you," he says. Then he shuffles a sort of tap dance back to his table.

"That guy's too much," Duckie says. "I think he likes you!"

You can feel your face turning red. Just then Giovanni comes to your table. You hope he does not notice the color of your face.

(continued on page 20)

"What would you like to eat?" he asks. "Our specialties are the *risotto di pesce, calamari fritti,* and *zuppa di pesce.*"

"We'll tell you in a minute," says Duckie. He walks to the other table.

"I don't understand a thing," you tell Duckie. "And I really would like to know how much things cost before I order. I didn't bring much money with me. This place looks expensive. Don't they believe in menus? Besides, we agreed to a free Coke. We didn't agree to buy dinner."

"The choices are rice with seafood, fried octopus, and fish soup," says Duckie. "And I don't have much money either. Maybe we should go."

If you leave, turn to page 50.

If you order, turn to page 58.

LOTS OF BOYS!

You decide that being late is much worse than showing up in pink. Besides, you only got the job a few hours ago, what does she expect? So, you put on a pink shirt and leave for work.

"Hi," you say to Maggie when you walk into the empty restaurant. "I'm sorry about the shirt, but I didn't have time to buy one."

"Don't worry about it," she says. "You can pick one up later. Come on, I'll show you what to do before the rush begins."

"Hey, I think we should all wear pink shirts!" says a tall dark-haired boy as he comes out from behind the counter. "Maybe we should wear pink bows in our hair, too." He dances in a circle like a ballerina.

"Oh, Chuckles, you would look simply divine in pink," says a blond boy with freckles and bright blue eyes.

You can't help laughing.

"All right, guys. That's enough!" Maggie says. She looks at you. "The only trouble you'll have with this job is dealing with Chuck and Russell, your co-workers!"

The two guys curtsey and return to work. You listen as Maggie shows you how to work the cash register, take orders, and clear dishes. Every time you look at the boys, they wave or make weird faces at you.

(continued on page 22)

You also meet Denise, a tall, skinny girl with stringy brown hair tied in a tight pony tail.

"Hi," you say when you are introduced.

"Hello," Denise says quietly. Then she turns away from you and stares at the floor.

Friendly, isn't she, you think.

"Hi, Denise," you hear Chuck say in a mocking tone. Denise doesn't respond.

Within the next twenty minutes, customers begin piling in. Denise works the cash register while you and Chuck and Russell wait tables.

The evening goes well. Whenever you get confused or can't answer a question, one of the guys always seems to be there to help you out.

For the next week, you work every day. You quickly get used to the routine; and although it is hard work, you are really enjoying it! Chuck and Russell are wacky and fun. You are amazed at how well you know them after only a few days. Denise, however, is another story. You try to be friendly, but she just does her job and talks to you only when necessary.

On Friday night the restaurant is packed. As you are rushing around like a madwoman trying to keep all your orders straight and all your customers happy, you keep glancing toward one corner of the restaurant. There, sitting by himself, is a spectacular-looking, dark-haired guy with the most beautiful smile and a golden tan. Russell, unfortunately, has

(continued on page 23)

LOTS OF BOYS! 23

the guy's table; and when the guy gets up to leave, you are sure you will never see him again.

What a waste, you think as he walks out the door. Then you notice a camera hanging on the chair where he was sitting. You go over to pick it up. Russell sees you.

"Oh, brother!" Russell says. "What a dingbat Greg is!"

"You know him?" you say.

"Oh, yeah, he comes in all the time," says Russell. "I'm sure he'll come in tomorrow when he realizes the camera is missing."

You look at the camera. There is a label on the strap with an address on it: 463 West Grove Street, Apt. 6.

Wow, you think, your mind racing, *I pass by there on my way home.*

If you offer to take the camera to Greg after work tonight, turn to page 27.

If you let Russell deal with it, turn to page 109.

You look at Russell. You look at the glass. You look at the woman. It is very tempting, but in the end you bring her an ordinary glass of water. A part of you wishes you had had more guts. If anyone deserves a dribble glass, this woman does.

She finally leaves, and you have about five minutes before the place is packed again.

"They finish breakfast, and then they want lunch," Russell says. "Don't they know that the surgeon general has determined that eating is dangerous to your health?"

You laugh and run off to seat a family of five.

"Meet me in the back room in ten minutes, baby!" Russell jokes as you rush by him with a spinach salad.

Five minutes later he steps up to you in the kitchen.

"We must stop meeting like this," he says, reaching his hand behind your head as though he is preparing to give you a passionate kiss.

"Shhh," you say. "I think I hear my husband!"

You are both exhausted by the time the lunch bunch leaves. Russell plops down at a table, and you join him.

"I've come to a major breakthrough in technology," Russell says. "A big step for mankind!"

"What?" you ask.

"It's what we've all been waiting for," he continues.

"Well, tell me," you say.

(continued on page 25)

"Are you ready?" he says.

"Russell . . ." you say.

"This major breakthrough is a waiter's and waitress's dream!" You look at the excited gleam in his eyes. "Motorized shoes!" he yells. "Just think, we could make millions."

"Oh, brother," you say.

"Hey," says Russell. "Do you have any plans for tomorrow?"

"Nope," you say.

"How about going hiking?" he says.

"I'd love to," you say.

Russell smiles and takes your hand. He looks into your eyes without saying a word. You feel goose bumps.

"Great," he says after what seems like forever.

That night, Russell calls.

"How about if I pick you up at 8:30," he says.

"Sounds super," you say.

"Terrific! I can't wait to see you," he says in a soft, slow voice.

You just saw me! you think. Then you realize that you are excited about seeing him too . . . even though you just left each other a few hours ago.

About two seconds later the phone rings again. You pick it up.

"Hi, beautiful," Chuck says. "What's up?"

You talk for a few minutes, giving him a rundown on the day.

"So what are the plans for tomorrow?" he says.

(continued on page 26)

Suddenly you realize that you have been picturing tomorrow without Chuck. You have been imagining hiking with Russell . . . just the two of you. Your head begins to spin. You know that every Monday has been threesome day. You begin to wonder if it was something Russell said that gave you the impression it was going to be just the two of you.

"Have you talked to Russell?" you ask.

"Nope, called you first," he says.

If you tell Chuck the plans, turn to page 62.

If you don't, turn to page 46.

LOTS OF BOYS!

"Listen, I'll take the camera by his house. It's on my way home," you tell Russell. You see this as the perfect opportunity to meet this cute guy.

And of course he'll be so thankful that he'll take me to dinner and we'll live happily ever after, you chuckle to yourself.

"If you want," Russell says. "But I'm sure he'll come back for it tomorrow."

"No, really, it's no problem!" you insist, wondering if Russell can see through your offer.

"Fine with me," says Russell.

At 9:30, you get off work. You go into the bathroom, fix your make-up, brush your hair, and rush out the door. You walk to 463 West Grove and find apartment 6. Your heart is beating fast as you take a deep breath and knock on the door.

A short, petite girl with curly blond hair answers the door. Your heart drops.

His girlfriend? His sister? you wonder.

"Is, uh, Greg here?" you ask.

"No one is here," she answers. "I'm visiting my boyfriend, but I haven't seen a soul. I don't even know who Greg is. He's probably one of my boyfriend's roommates. I haven't met them all."

That knocks off girlfriend and sister, you think happily.

"Well, he left his camera at my restaurant. Will you give it to him?"

(continued on page 28)

"Sure," she says. "I'm leaving tomorrow morning; if I don't see him, I'll leave a note with the camera."

"Thanks," you say. "I appreciate it."

"No problem," the girl says.

A lot of good that did, you think as you walk home. *I would have been better off waiting to see him tomorrow. Oh well.*

The next day, you have the lunch hour shift. The place is packed, and you and Chuck are the only ones working. Denise and Russell are due any minute. You are cleaning off a table when you see Greg walk in.

You stop short, barely catching the plate that flies to the edge of your tray. *He's probably coming in to thank me,* you think, brushing your hair back quickly with your hand. You casually walk over to him.

"Hi," you say.

"Hi," Greg says. *What a great smile!* "Listen," he continues, "I was here yesterday and I left a camera at my table. I hope you have it."

Your stomach feels weak. "Didn't you get it?" you say. "Have you been home?"

"Yes, of course I've been home," he says with a puzzled look on his face. "Why?"

"I brought it over to West Grove Street last night and gave it to your roommate's girlfriend."

(continued on page 29)

"West Grove Street!" he says. "I don't live there any more!"

Oh, no, you think. *What have I done?*

"I better get over there now," he says, walking quickly toward the door.

If you go with him, turn to page 51.

If you let him go alone, turn to page 56.

"Russell," you say. "I'll do it for you if you really want me to. But I think you're making a mistake."

"I just can't face Maggie," he says. "Tell her that I'll pay back every penny."

"But wouldn't you feel better about yourself if *you* explained it to her? I know she'd understand."

"Look, if you don't want to do it, just tell me. I'll write a letter when I get to Washington."

"Something tells me that this is all wrong," you say. "But if you really want me to, I'll do it."

"Thanks!" he says. "It really does mean a lot to me."

He hugs you.

"You know," he says, "I really value our friendship. We've known each other for such a short time, but I feel as if I've known you forever."

You smile. "Me too."

Russell puts his arms around you and brings you close.

"I'm not sure friendship is the right word," he says, kissing you on the lips.

Suddenly you realize how much he means to you. You know you will miss him terribly while he is gone. For a few minutes you sit in silence, holding each other. You have never felt so close to anyone before.

"I guess I'd better go," he says. "I have a lot of things to do tonight before I fly out tomorrow."

"Will you write?"

(continued on page 31)

"Yes," he says as he gets up and walks to the door. He is holding your hand so tightly that you feel as though you are attached to him.

"I hope your father is all right," you say.

"Thanks," he says. "Thanks for everything. You're the best friend anyone could ask for."

He kisses you again and leaves.

"Have a good flight," you call as he walks away.

You sit at the kitchen table with your head in your hands.

Did I do the right thing, you wonder. Something inside you answers no. *He's not going to be able to live with himself. He should have been the one to tell Maggie.*

But you know it is too late.

When you get to work the next day you explain everything to Maggie.

"You know," she says. "I'm really disappointed in Russell. It's bad enough that he stole the money, but he could at least have come in and told me himself."

You have to agree.

A week later you receive a letter from Russell with a check for $150:

> I want you to know how much you mean to me and how much I really appreciate all your help. My father is improving, and the doctors say he will be all right.
>
> I am not returning to Colorado. I will truly miss

(continued on page 32)

you, but I just can't face the scene of my crime. It would be a constant reminder of an awful time in my life. Please try to understand.

Take care.

With all my love,
Russell

You will always wonder if it might have been different if you had insisted that Russell go to Maggie himself.

The End

LOTS OF BOYS!

The more you think about it, the more you are convinced that Russell should be the one to deal with Maggie.

It'll make him feel even worse if I do it for him, you think.

You are still holding him in your arms as you steel yourself to say what you have to say. You are shaking.

"I can't," you say. "I can't be the one to tell her. You have to do that for yourself."

He releases himself from your arms.

"But I thought you were my friend," he says.

"Oh, Russell, I am. And that's why I can't do it for you."

"Thanks a lot," he says and walks toward the door.

You bite your lip and close your eyes.

Be strong, you tell yourself. *You have to be strong. It's the right decision. I know it is!*

"Russell?" you say as he opens the door.

He turns to face you. You can see the pain in his face.

"I already said thank you," he mutters. The door shuts.

The next day you are sitting at the breakfast table staring at the omelette in front of you. You can't eat. You couldn't sleep, either. All night long you kept wondering if you did the right thing.

What kind of a friend am I? you kept asking yourself.

(continued on page 34)

There is a knock on the door. You open it and Russell is standing there with a smile and a rose.

"I did it," he says. "And I feel so much better about myself. Maggie is going to let me keep the job. We made a deal, and she's going to take it out of my paycheck."

He put his hand on your shoulder and looks into your eyes.

"Thank you. I can't tell you how much this means to me."

Russell puts his arms around you and pulls you toward him. His lips meet yours, and you feel a warmth throughout your body. There are tears in your eyes. But this time they are tears of joy.

The End

"Siamo di Milano," Duckie says. Then very slowly, and with an Italian accent, "We—are—from—Milano!"

You have to fight to keep from laughing.

"United—States," he says to you, pointing to himself. "Wow! Hey, Mark, come here," he says. "We're finally going to get to meet some Italian girls." He turns to you. "I—am—John." he says slowly. He points to his friend. "Mark."

"I—am—happy—to—meet—you," you say haltingly in your best Italian accent. "I—am—Giovanna." You point to Duckie. "Patrizia."

Duckie whispers to you. "We aren't going to get away with this. Let's tell them we were just kidding."

You turn to tell them, but as you open your mouth, John points to three friends who have just walked over.

"To—ny, Bill, Ka—ren," he says, enunciating carefully. And then, "Su—san, Ti—mo—thy, Steve. These girls are from Milan, Italy," he tells them.

You are now surrounded by the entire group of Americans; they are all fascinated by you and Duckie.

"You—speak—very—good—English," says one of the boys.

"I — wish — I — could — speak — Italian," says another.

(continued on page 36)

"I—buy—you—*gelato*," says John, gesturing as he talks.

You look at his deep green eyes that crinkle when he smiles. He is so sweet. You are furious at yourself for getting into this. It would have been fun to get to know him; now you are trapped in your own game.

"Talk—in—Italian," says John. "It—is—such—a—pretty—language."

Duckie jabbers something you do not understand.

"My—family—is—Italian," John says to you. "Isn't my name *Giovanni* in Italian?"

Oh, no, you think, realizing that you don't have a clue.

Duckie jumps in, "Yes—that—is—right."

"I—would—like—to—know—you—better, Giovanna," says John to you. "Can—I—buy—you—dinner—tomorrow?"

You would like to know him better, too. But you don't dare say yes. You know you could never pull it off for a whole night, and you don't want to make him feel like a fool by telling him what you have done.

"My—parents—would—not—permit—that," you say sadly.

"I—am—sad—that—you—live—so—far—away. Will—you—write—to—me? I—would—like—to—see—you—again," John says.

(continued on page 37)

"Me—too," you say, as he hands you a piece of paper with his address. You look at the paper and discover that he lives in Miami, Florida, about ten minutes from where you live. You are furious at yourself as he kisses both your cheeks in the Italian custom. Then, as he walks out the door, you hear him say to his friend, "You know, there's something about Italian women that is so different from Americans. They're so much more sincere and honest."

The End

You race out the door and jog all the way into town. About two blocks from the restaurant you see a secondhand clothing store. You run in.

Frantically, you flip through racks of blouses. Then you go through the piles of clothes on the tables. Nothing. Not a single white, short-sleeved shirt.

You run next door into a big discount store and race through the shampoos and hardware and paper goods until you reach the clothes. At first you see only children's things; then you see the adult clothing. The blouses are packaged flat in cellophane and are lying on shelves. You have to read the labels in order to determine if they are short-sleeved. In a panic, you begin flipping through the blouses. You cannot even find a plain white blouse, let alone a short-sleeved one.

You run out the door and on into a small shop that is blaring rock music. You know immediately that they probably don't have what you are looking for, but you ask anyway. You were right.

Now you are panicky. You are already half an hour late, and you still don't have the blouse. You run down the street in search of other stores. You run into several of them, but no one has your short-sleeved blouse. The salesladies all try to talk you into something else, and you are ready to scream.

(continued on page 39)

LOTS OF BOYS! 39

Finally, you look at your watch and discover that you are 45 minutes late. You cannot look any more. You run to the restaurant. Sweaty and out of breath, you walk through the door.

"Come over here," says Maggie.

You walk over.

"I'm sure you have a good excuse, but I run a business here, and even good excuses aren't good enough for me. You're fired. You can return the pants tomorrow."

I really blew it, you think as you walk out the door.

The End

"Patrizia!" you yell, taking the bandana out of your stringy hair.

"Ciao!" she yells back, waving. "What number do you live?"

You call down your apartment number and tell her to come up. You rush into the bathroom, wash your face, and attempt to do something with your hair.

Hopeless, you think as you hear the knock on the door.

Patrizia walks in followed by the boy. She introduces you to her brother, Masimo. She is all smiles as she explains that she has lost your address and phone number.

"I only remember the street," she says. "So we walk up and down to find you."

Masimo says something in Italian.

"Si. Si," Patrizia says, and then she turns to you. "My brother works tonight on a gondola. There is a celebration on water tonight. There are many lights that we put in the sky. I do not know in English."

"Fireworks," you say.

"Yes. This is it," Patrizia continues. "He asks us on his boat to see this fireworks. You want to come?"

"Of course!" you say enthusiastically. You and Patrizia make plans to meet Masimo in an hour at the dock, and he leaves.

(continued on page 41)

LOTS OF BOYS! 41

Patrizia waits as you quickly wash your hair and change. Then the two of you head out to San Marco. As you walk through the streets, you pass by the caffè you have been going to every day. Suddenly you remember all of your frustration when the waiters talk about you in Italian. If you went in with Patrizia, and she pretended that she was American too, she could tell you what they were saying.

If you ask her to pretend she is American, turn to page 115.

If you keep walking, turn to page 90.

You jump up and walk away. *Please don't follow me,* you think. Your heart is pounding. *Why am I so scared? He was probably just being friendly.*

Nevertheless, you keep walking until you are far from the dock. Finally, you turn around. There is no sign of the painter. You sigh in relief and feel your body relax.

It is definitely time to go home, you think.

You work your way toward your house, and a smile spreads across your face when you see the familiar building. You are about to enter when you remember that your mother had asked you to pick up some orange juice.

You walk to a small market that you just passed. You search the store for juices. Nothing.

An older woman says something in Italian to you.

"Orange juice?" you say.

She tilts her head and shrugs her shoulders. You try again.

"Orange? Fruit?" You make a circular shape with your hands.

"Ah," the woman cries. *"Ho capito."*

She goes to the back of the store and comes back with a big smile on her face. She is holding an apple.

You shake your head. You can feel a lump forming in your throat and tears beginning to fill your eyes.

Why doesn't she understand? you think. You motion drinking. Still no response.

(continued on page 43)

LOTS OF BOYS!

You look around once more. A girl about your age is putting lettuce, cookies, and salami on the counter. As she picks out a cheese, she talks loudly with the woman. They both laugh. You are sure they are laughing at you.

You stand there frustrated, looking blankly at the shelves that you have already searched, pretending that you know what you are doing.

I feel like such an idiot. I can't even shop! I hate this! you think.

You watch as the woman takes money from the girl. Then the girl heads for the door.

If you ask the girl for help, turn to page 101.

If you don't want to ask her, turn to page 86.

You look at your filthy shorts and your baggy T-shirt. You know that your hair is a disaster.

No way! you think. *She's with a guy, too. How embarrassing!*

You watch her walk down the street and out of sight.

Oh, well, you think. *I'll see her when she calls.*

For the next week you wait for a call. Whenever you come home, you hope for a message. Nothing.

After two weeks you give up on getting a phone call and look for her in the street; but you never do see her.

You have been undone by vanity.

The End

Marzio returns. "Let's go," he says, enthusiastically taking your hand and pulling you toward the gondola at the front of the line.

You have been standing there, first on one foot, then on the other, agonizing over your feet. When Marzio yanks, you lose your balance and go down.

At first, you are only embarrassed, sprawled out on the dock like an idiot. But when you get up, you are devastated. You cannot walk; you have sprained your ankle.

You wish you could disappear and start this night all over again. As Marzio and the gondola man carry you to the doctor, there are tears rolling down your cheeks. You have just ruined the most wonderful night of your life.

The End

"I'm not sure of any plans," you say.

"Well, if any wonderful ideas pop into your head, give me a call."

When you hang up the phone, your hand is shaking. *I've never lied to him before,* you think. *What if Russell tells him?* Then you decide that you really didn't lie. Actually, you *don't* know where you're going.

The next day, you get up earlier than usual and you try on three pairs of shorts before deciding to wear the lavender ones. You've never cared what you were wearing when you were with Russell. Never, until now.

At 8:30 sharp, a horn honks outside your house. You open the door, not knowing whether you are going to see one or two guys. There sits Russell, alone, beaming a smile at you. You are relieved and excited. You can feel your entire body smiling back.

"Good morning," he says. "Have I got plans for us!"

He drives for about fifteen minutes until you reach a wooded area that has several dirt paths leading into the forest. Russell parks the car and slips into a backpack.

"Lunch," he explains.

As you walk down a narrow path, you are surrounded by huge trees. Off to the left, between the

(continued on page 47)

LOTS OF BOYS! 47

tree trunks, you can see a river sparkling in the sunlight.

"Me Tarzan, you Jane," shouts Russell, jumping up and swinging from a tree branch.

You tickle him, and he lets go and chases you up the hill. When he catches you, you both tumble down and roll into a blackberry bush, prickles and all.

You are on your back, laughing, when Russell sits up next to you. He puts his arms on either side of you and looks into your eyes.

"I'm so glad I know you," he says, sounding almost shy. Then he pops up and grabs your hand.

"Come on!" He pulls you up. "We've got some climbing to do."

You walk for another fifteen minutes until you reach a large, rocky mountain.

"Let's go up there," he says, pointing to the top of the mountain.

"No problem," you say. "I'll just jog up."

Russell takes your hand and leads you up the easy part. Then you come to the part where you need two hands and two feet. Carefully, you make your way up the rocky slope, searching all the time for your next foothold.

This is not what I was hoping for, you think, as the mountain gets steeper and steeper. Every once

(continued on page 48)

in a while you come upon a rock with a crevice in the middle. Using two hands and two feet, you straddle the crevice and inch your way up.

"Did anyone ever tell you that you make a beautiful mountain goat?" Russell says from about ten feet up.

"Not recently," you say, panting and trying to keep up with him.

Finally, you catch up. Actually, Russell stops on the top of a ledge and you stop underneath it. The incline is vertical, and you have no idea how he got up there. You raise both arms and can just about touch the bottom of the ledge.

"Come on!" he says, reaching over the ledge for your arms. "Grab on to me and I'll pull. You just walk your feet up the wall."

You look up at the rocky slope. It goes straight up for about eight feet. Russell is stretched out on the ledge at the top, holding his hands out to you.

You have never tried to climb anything like that before. One voice inside your head keeps saying, "Go for it!" Another answers, "No way!"

If you go for it, turn to page 74.

If you don't, turn to page 15.

LOTS OF BOYS! 49

You look at Giovanni. *How can we leave?* you think. *We just got here.*

"He's right," you say to Duckie. "We really have to see the other islands."

"OK," Duckie says.

"Ah, you are very smart!" Giovanni says. "It was not even a question!"

You thank the photographers and say good-bye. Then you wander around Burano for another hour and go to the dock to wait for the boat to the next island.

As you are waiting, you hear a loud, shrill voice screaming at everyone in English. You look over and see a short, slightly heavy American girl. She sees you.

"Americans!" she screams. "Thank God!" She runs over to you. "These people don't know anything, and nobody speaks a word of English. Can you speak Italian?"

You wish you could crawl into a hole. You certainly don't want to be associated with her.

"Yes," says Duckie. "I do."

"Well, then I'll just stay with you for the rest of the day," she screams. "I'm so happy to see Americans!"

You look around. Everyone is staring at her. You are suddenly embarrassed to be American.

Why didn't we go on the boat with the photographers? you think.

The End

"Duckie," you whisper when Giovanni leaves, "we can't stay here and eat. I would die if we didn't have enough money to pay for lunch."

"Yeah, I guess you're right. But those photographers are so nice. It would be a great way to meet some Italians without picking them up on the street," says Duckie.

Giovanni returns. "Are you ready to experience my wonderful food?" he asks.

"We are very sorry," you say, "but we cannot stay to eat. We must catch a boat for Murano. We are meeting my mother there in just a little while."

"Thank you for the Cokes," says Duckie.

"Oh, *ragazze,* you must not leave! I will miss your smiling faces!"

"We are sorry too," says Duckie.

"And I'm sure Fulvio Rossino will be very sad too. He wanted to welcome you to our country by paying for your meal. *Che peccato!* What a pity!"

"*Si,*" you say to Duckie as you walk out the door. "*Che peccato!*"

The End

LOTS OF BOYS!

You rush over to Chuck and quickly explain what has happened. "I've got to go with him," you say.

"You're kidding," he yells, pointing at the crowd. Then he looks at the panic in your face. "All right, go ahead. But hurry back."

You rush out the door. "Greg, wait! I'm going with you."

"Come on, then," he says, getting in his car.

You open the door and jump in. You barely have time to introduce yourself as Greg speeds to West Grove Street. You follow him up the stairs, and he knocks on the door.

A big, muscular guy about twenty-five answers the door.

"Yes?" he says.

"I left a camera here yesterday by mistake," you say. "I've come to get it."

"I haven't seen any camera," he says.

"A girl took it," you say, anxiously.

"Well," he says. "I haven't seen it."

Greg looks at you. Your eyes begin to water.

"I gave it to a blond girl, she said . . ."

"Hey, Andy," says the guy. "Have you seen a camera around here?"

An even bigger guy with a blond crew cut comes to the door. "Uh, uh. I haven't seen a thing."

"Look!" Greg says. "She left the camera here and we want it back."

(continued on page 52)

"Hey, Mac, I told you, I don't know what you're talking about," says the first guy. "Excuse me." He slams the door in your face.

You are too shaken to move. "Greg, I . . ."

"I believe you," he says. "Those guys are lying through their teeth. Shhhh." He puts his hand over your mouth and his ear up to the door. You are shaking as you listen through the door.

"That wasn't so hard," says a voice from inside. "And we've got ourselves a neat camera."

"Yeah, but I think we better get it out of here, just in case they come back."

"They won't be back," says the first voice. "They were pretty intimidated."

"You're probably right, but let's get it out anyway."

You and Greg walk quietly down the stairs and out of the building.

"I want to catch them with the camera in their hands," says Greg.

"But, Greg, they're so much bigger than we are," you say.

"Let's just see what happens," says Greg, leading you behind a thick hedge in front of the house next door.

You can feel the sweat building up on your forehead as you watch them walk out the door. One of them is carrying a brown paper bag. They pass by your bush and walk to an old blue Pontiac that is

(continued on page 53)

parked about twenty feet from where you are watching. The blond guy opens the door, puts the bag inside, and locks up. Then they both get into a blue Mustang and drive away.

You and Greg run out.

"How are we going to get it now!" he mumbles, trying all the locked doors.

"I know," you say. "Wait here."

You run to the nearest house and knock on the door. After a brief conversation with the woman who answers, you return with a wire hanger.

"I'm famous for locking my keys in the car!" you say. Within fifteen minutes, you have opened the door. Greg grabs the paper bag and pulls out his camera.

"We did it!" he screams, hugging you. You are both laughing as you get into his car and drive away. "This deserves a celebration. How about dinner tonight, on me?"

"Dinner sounds great," you say, relieved and excited. "But it's definitely on me!"

The End

You decide that this guy is really cute, and you wouldn't mind getting to know him. He's obviously interested in you. You'd better not try to put him on.

"We're American," you say, and you introduce yourself.

"Yeah, now that I look at you again, you do look American."

At that moment a gang of about twenty Americans piles into Caffè Roma.

"We're on a tour," says John, turning toward the crowd. "It was nice meeting you."

You watch as he disappears into the crowd.

Hmm, you think. *I was only interesting while he thought I was Italian.*

You look over at Dario and wonder if he likes you just because you're American.

"Bambolina!" he yells when you catch his eye. "Please, I need you."

You walk over to the counter.

"No, I need you back here. You must help me to make the *gelati*. It is so many people, and Piero takes a break."

You and Duckie jump behind the counter and begin taking orders from the Americans. *Cioccolato! Fragola! Panna! Gianduia! Bacio! Zabaglone!* You have been coming here often enough to know every flavor, and you answer all the Americans' questions. You are not nearly as skilled at dishing out the ice cream.

(continued on page 55)

LOTS OF BOYS!

By the time the rush dies down, you and Duckie look psychedelic. Your shirt is covered in chocolate, berry, and practically every other flavor. Dario looks at you.

"My rainbow *bambolina!*" he says, hugging you. "I am so happy you are here. I thank you very much."

You kiss him on both cheeks and wonder if he likes you because you are foreign or because you are you. You cannot really be sure.

Then you think, *Who cares?*

The End

"Hey, Miss! Can we have our soup?" calls a woman.

"Excuse me," calls another.

I can't leave now, you think. *Chuck would go crazy. There are too many people here.*

Greg rushes out the door and jumps into his car. You go back to the motions of waitressing: taking orders, delivering meals, filling water glasses. But your mind is on the camera.

"I'm sure he got it back," Chuck assures you.

Yeah, you tell yourself. *Of course he did.*

About ten minutes after he walked out the door, Greg walks back in. The expression on his face tells you that something is wrong.

"They don't have it!" he announces in an angry voice. "The guy said no one ever brought over a camera."

You are speechless. Finally, the words come out.

"But I brought it there. I did. I swear I did. I gave it to a blond girl, and she said she was visiting her boyfriend."

"Well . . ." says Greg. You notice that he is shaking. "They don't know anything about a blond girl . . . and they don't know anything about a camera."

"Now wait a minute," says Chuck. "Are you saying that she's lying about this? If she says she left it at the address that was on the camera, then that's what she did."

The noise level of the argument has drawn the attention of everyone in the restaurant.

(continued on page 57)

"Well, it's a $200 camera, and somebody's got to pay for it!" says Greg.

"*You* left it here," says Chuck.

"So I should pick it up from here!" says Greg.

I don't have $200, you think, as the tears run down your face.

"Chuck," you say. "It's OK. I really feel responsible for this. Let me take care of it."

You ask Greg to sit down with you and work out a solution. You promise to give him $50 every other week. That way, it will only take you two months to pay him off.

You know something is very wrong with the deal, but you really do feel responsible.

You also feel like a complete jerk!

The End

"Why don't we order one thing and split it," you say to Duckie. "Between us we can probably scrape up enough money to buy one meal."

"Good idea," says Duckie. "It would be a real insult if we walked out now."

Giovanni returns to your table. "*Allora,* ladies, what would you take?"

"Well," says Duckie, "we're not very hungry, so we'll just have one *risotto di pesce.*"

"*Solamente un risotto?*" he yells, throwing his arms in the air. "*Non possibile! Non è abbastanza!*"

"He doesn't think we ordered enough," says Duckie.

"I figured that out," you respond. "He's having a heart attack over how little we ordered."

"And, uh," Duckie stumbles, "we'll have a salad too."

"*Mamma mia!*" says Giovanni, looking at the ceiling and gesturing with his hands.

You and Duckie sit silently, not knowing what to do. Suddenly, as if on cue, you burst out laughing.

Fulvio Rossino walks over to your table. "You have ordered?" he asks.

"Yes," you say. "We are not very hungry, so we ordered only one course and one salad for both of us."

"I see," he says. "Girls cannot live that way. You must eat more." He leaves you and walks toward the kitchen.

(continued on page 59)

LOTS OF BOYS!

A few minutes later two huge bowls of rice with seafood are brought to your table, along with a basket of bread. You are sure there is enough rice to feed six people. You and Duckie just stare at it.

"I think they're worried that we might be starving," says Duckie.

"Right. We do look malnourished," you say, patting your stomach that is still full from the night before.

The dish is wonderful: fish, clams, and shrimp mixed with rice in a garlic and wine base. You are stuffed before you are half-finished.

Giovanni comes to your table. "You don't like?" he says when he sees your bowl.

"I love it," you say and begin to eat again. You do not want to offend him, so you finish everything.

"Ah," he says with a big smile as he takes your bowl. Two seconds later he arrives holding a huge platter loaded with whole fish. He puts a fish on each of your plates.

"But . . ." you say.

"Eat," he says, and he takes the rest of the fish to the table of photographers.

You look over at the other table. Dario stands up and waves at you.

Oh my gosh, you think. *This is embarrassing!* You quickly turn back and look at Duckie.

Rossino walks over to your table. "The food is good, yes?"

(continued on page 60)

"The food is wonderful," you say, forcing it down. You have never eaten so much in your life.

Next they bring you salad and cheese, and then special Burano cookies and ice cream and coffee. You cannot believe all the food, and you have no idea how you are going to pay for it.

"We could always wash dishes," says Duckie.

"For the rest of our lives," you say, dreading the arrival of the bill.

You watch as Giovanni hands Rossino a bill and then accepts the photographer's money. The group gets up to go. You try to sneak a last look at Dario, but there is no sneaking. He is looking at you and your eyes meet. You both smile.

"Well," says Duckie, "the news isn't going to get any better. Let's face it." She waves to Giovanni.

"How much do we owe you?" you ask, crossing your fingers that it's not too much.

"Niente!" he says, gesturing toward the photography group.

"That means nothing," says Duckie. "They must have paid for us."

"Can we accept it?" you ask.

"We have no choice," says Duckie. "Thank you," she calls to Rossino.

"Grazie," you call to the group, not certain if it was Rossino or the group who paid your bill.

Rossino smiles at you and nods his head. Then he walks over to you. "Now we go back to Venice on our boat. Would you like to come with us?"

(continued on page 61)

Dario is standing behind him, nodding his head and making faces of encouragement.

"Wow," says Duckie. "Our own private boat!"

"But we've just begun our tour. I'm not sure I want to go back to Venice," you say. "What do you think?"

"What I think?" says Giovanni, interrupting. "What I think is you cannot go back before you see the islands. It would be an insult to me, Giovanni."

If you join the photographers, turn to page 70.

If you go on with your tour, turn to page 49.

"Well, um. We did make some plans. But Russell's the camp director," you say. "Call him."

"Right-o," says Chuck. "See you around campus."

At 8:30 the next morning, the two guys arrive together. Chuck knows of a fantastic hiking trail that ends in a beautiful picnic spot. The path is just wide enough for the three of you to walk along with your arms around each other. Soon, you begin to sing and do a Laverne-and-Shirley walk.

By noon you are starved, but the guys insist upon marching onward. At 12:30 the narrow path ends and you are suddenly at the edge of a beautiful lake.

"I'm going fishing!" Chuck says, taking off his shoes and shirt and diving into the pond.

"Wait for me!" Russell says, following.

"Why didn't you guys tell me there was swimming," you say. "I didn't even bring a suit."

"Suits are not required," says Chuck. "You can swim in shorts and a shirt. And of course, if you don't want to get your clothes wet, you can always . . ."

"Oh, shut up," you scream, diving in with your clothes on.

When you all come out of the water Russell unpacks a picnic basket: turkey sandwiches, potato salad, and fruit. Chuck, as usual, is very talkative and hyperactive. Russell, however, is acting a bit strange. It almost seems as if he is annoyed at you. By the end of the day you wonder if you made a

(continued on page 63)

mistake in telling Chuck that you and Russell had plans.

For the next few days you work day shifts with Chuck, and you barely see Russell. Chuck tells you that Russell seems a little weird lately.

"He's just not as crazy as he used to be. He's not even fun. Last night he wouldn't even go bowling with me!"

"I'm sure he'll get over it," you say, wondering if Russell's mood has something to do with your including Chuck on Monday.

On Saturday, you work alone with Russell.

"Hi, handsome, long time no see," you say when he walks in.

"Hi," is all he says.

Can he really still be mad at me? you wonder.

"So what have you been up to?" you ask.

"Oh, nothing," Russell says, and he goes over to help a customer.

For the rest of the day, he barely talks to you. He seems to be constantly busy, even when there is nothing to do.

"What's wrong, Russ," you ask. "Can I help?"

"Nothing!" he says.

That night you call Chuck.

"He's the same way with me," Chuck says. "So don't think it's something you've done."

On Monday, you and Chuck go sailing. On Tuesday, Russell works the evening shift with Denise.

Wednesday morning, Maggie calls a meeting.

(continued on page 64)

"Kids, I'm not sure how to say this, so I'm going to say it straight out. $150 was missing from yesterday's cash receipts. Does anyone know what happened to it?"

Your first thought is, *Denise did it,* and then you are angry with yourself for thinking it. Even though you have not become friends, you feel sorry for her. Recently, Russell told you that he had learned that Denise's mother had died four years ago, and fourteen-year-old Denise became a mother to her three younger brothers and sisters. She cooks, cleans, goes to school plays, and even helps her father out with the money she earns. She has had no time for a life of her own. You don't really like her, but you feel a special kind of understanding and compassion for her.

"I don't have a clue," you say in answer to Maggie's question. Chuck and Russell and Denise shrug their shoulders.

"I'd like to talk to you individually," Maggie says. "Denise, you first."

You all watch silently as they go in the back.

"I bet she took it," Chuck says.

"She's been working the register," you say.

Russell breaks in. "Why would she take it? She's been working here for two years. You can't accuse somebody because you don't like her. I bet it was one of the freaky customers we get in here."

Maggie sees you one at a time. When Denise

(continued on page 65)

LOTS OF BOYS! 65

leaves for the day, Maggie tells the rest of you that she is convinced that Denise did it.

"But do you have any proof?" Russell asks.

"Intuition," says Maggie. "I don't need proof."

"That's called circumstantial evidence," says Russell. "Our whole system of justice is set up to avoid the use of intuition."

You are rather proud of Russell for defending Denise; you know he doesn't like her.

You rush home after work to get ready for a big night. You have been spending so much time with Chuck and Russell that your mother is feeling left out of your life. You promised that tonight you would go out to dinner and the theatre with her. When you arrive home, she is fussing over what to wear. She is obviously all excited.

Just as you are going out the door, the phone rings.

"Hi," says Russell. "Can you meet me tonight? I'd like to talk to you." He sounds upset; his voice is shaking.

If you cancel your plans with your mother, turn to page 77.

If you tell Russell you are about to go out, turn to page 96.

It is 6:30. You are a nervous wreck, and your room is a disaster. Clothes are everywhere. You have tried on every pair of pants you own, three dresses, and two skirts. You finally decide on the first pair of pants you had on. You put on a white button-down blouse and a vest and move on to your make-up. Blue eye liner. No, gray. Maybe none.

"Nothing looks right," you scream, storming out of the bedroom.

Your mother assures you that you look gorgeous.

"You would say that if I weighed three hundred pounds and had shredded Levi's on!" you say. "What am I going to wear on my feet?"

"How about shoes?" says your mother.

"Oh, Mother," you say. "You're no help at all."

We might be doing a lot of walking, you think. You look at your flats sticking out from under the couch. Then you think, *But I look so much older in heels!*

You pick up the spiked pumps that you left in the kitchen last night and you put them on.

There is a knock on the door. Your stomach drops. You rush back into the bedroom and brush your hair for the hundredth time.

"Hello," you hear a male voice say. "I'm Marzio."

Do I really have to do this? you think as you walk into the living room. Then you see him: the dimples,

(continued on page 67)

LOTS OF BOYS!

the chocolate brown eyes, and the warm smile. You are mesmerized by his smile. He greets you, but you barely hear a word he says.

You kiss your mother good-bye and go off with Marzio. You decide that he is even better looking than he was yesterday.

"I think we have dinner at a small restaurant near here," he says. "That is good with you?"

"It sounds wonderful," you say.

"I am so happy to meet you tonight," he says.

Meet me tonight? you think. *What is he talking about?* You smile, confused.

You walk over a bridge and watch a gondola pass underneath.

"You have been on a gondola?" Marzio asks.

"No," you say.

He smiles, and you walk on, in and out of one tiny street after another. You are just beginning to regret having worn heels, when you come to a small restaurant on a corner overlooking a canal. Marzio opens the door, and you walk in.

"Ah, Signor Bandonelli! *Come va?*" says an older man with a white smock on. He puts his arm around you, winks at Marzio, and says, *"Bella ragazza!"*

You learned last night that this means beautiful girl.

There is a short conversation in Italian, and then you are led to a cozy table in the corner. There is an

(continued on page 68)

arrangement of gorgeous yellow flowers on the table and an unlit candle.

Marzio takes out a match and lights the candle. "You have beautiful eyes," he says. "They dance in the candlelight."

You feel as if you are going to melt right into your seat. You smile a thank you. He hands you a menu.

Spaghetti alla Amatriciana; Tortellini alla panna; Gnocchi al Pomodoro, you read, absolutely clueless as to what they are.

"What would you like?" Marzio asks.

Oh, no! What am I going to do? you think. *The only word I understand is spaghetti!*

"It all sounds so good," you say. "I can't decide."

"May I order for you?" Marzio says. "I know what is good."

"Oh, that sounds like a good idea!" you say. *It sounds like the only idea,* you think.

As you are waiting for the food, Marzio breaks off a flower, leans over, and puts it in your hair.

You feel yourself blushing.

During dinner, you and Marzio talk about your countries. You talk about how nice it is to meet people who are different from you. But the more you talk, the more you realize how much alike you really are. You discover that he writes poetry and you tell him about the secret book of poems that you have written. You have never told anyone about it before.

(continued on page 69)

LOTS OF BOYS!   69

"We are made for each other," says Marzio. He smiles, and his dimples deepen.

You cannot believe how comfortable you feel with him. You look out the window at the dimly lit street. The moon is reflected in the canal, and you see scattered couples walking hand in hand. Marzio reaches across the table and takes your hand.

This is not happening to me, you think. *I must be dreaming.*

When you leave the restaurant, Marzio puts his arm around you and you walk through the tiny streets. The only thing that keeps you from total ecstasy is your aching feet.

Marzio leads you to a dock where gondolas are lined up in the water. He leaves you for a moment and walks over and talks to an older man with a red and white straw hat on. As you stand waiting for him to finish, you can feel the pain in your feet.

Stupid heels, you think. *I wonder if I should just take them off?*

If you take off your shoes, turn to page 104.

If you leave them on, turn to page 45.

"When are we ever going to get a chance like this again?" Duckie says. "Our own private boat! We might even get some tips on photography. This guy is the most famous photographer in Italy. Let's go with them."

You have no trouble agreeing as you glance over at Dario. Something about his craziness really attracts you. He tilts his head, opens his eyes wide, and waits for your answer.

"OK," you say, holding in your enthusiasm. "We'd love to come."

Dario pokes a tall, blond-haired boy standing next to him. They both smile. You hadn't even noticed the other guy. *He's kind of cute,* you think.

You thank the owner again and follow the group of students toward the dock. They do not walk in a group. Instead, they scatter all over the place shooting pictures nonstop. One girl lies on the ground as she tries to get a unique angle for her shot of hanging laundry. A guy stands on a cement block to give him greater height.

You are carrying a 35mm camera too, but you are too embarrassed to take a picture with all these pro-photographers around snapping like crazy. You just learned how to use your camera, and it takes you forever to focus.

Everyone finally meets up at the dock next to a black speedboat. Rossino motions for you to get on. The rest follow.

(continued on page 71)

LOTS OF BOYS! 71

You sit in the back of the boat, facing the sun. Duckie sits on one side of you, Dario on the other. Dario takes out a big straw hat with ragged edges from under the seat and he puts it on your head.

"There is much sun!" he says.

Duckie looks at you and starts laughing.

"You are having a good vacation?" he says, struggling with the English. You can't help laughing when you look at him.

"Fantastic," you respond, trying to keep a straight face. "But it is not a vacation. I will be here for a year."

"A year!" Dario says with a big smile. "That is good. I can show to you Venice." You picture yourself walking around with this nut with Mickey Mouse sunglasses on.

"I would like that," you say out loud. *I think,* you say to yourself.

You look over at Duckie. She is talking to the blond guy.

"Venice is very beautiful," you say.

Dario looks deeply into your eyes. "Very beautiful, yes. Very beautiful, like you."

Uh, oh, you think. *What am I supposed to say to that?* You look at your shoes and say nothing.

A few minutes later Rossino says something to the group in Italian. All the photographers rush to the side of the boat and take pictures of the water. Then they rush to the other side and shoot some

(continued on page 72)

more. It looks like something out of a slapstick comedy, and you and Duckie can't stop laughing.

The water is sparkling with reflected sunlight. There are sailboats scattered on the water. You close your eyes and daydream in the warm rays.

"Let's go to the castle!" says one of the girls in Italian. Duckie translates for you.

"Non è possibile," says another. *"Devo ritornare a Venezia adesso."*

You are pleased that you understand what she has said: It is not possible. I have to return to Venice now.

"Anche' io," says a boy. Me, too.

"All right," says Rossino in Italian. "We will first go to Venice and then we will go on to the castle." This has to be translated for you.

"Where do you go tonight?" Dario asks you.

"I don't know," you say.

"I like that you come to my work," he says. "I work at Caffè Roma, *una gelateria*. The best *gelati* anywhere!"

"What is *gelati*?" you ask.

"What is *gelati*?" screams Dario. "I cannot believe you do not know *gelati!* Non è possibile!"

"It's Italian ice cream," says Duckie.

"Maybe I will come," you say.

"No maybe," he says. "I will wait for you."

You cannot get used to the Italian way. It feels very strange to hear boys so open about their feelings.

(continued on page 73)

LOTS OF BOYS! 73

Dario is more than just a good-looking flatterer. You learn in your conversation that he is eighteen years old and a photography student who lives in Venice.

This could be a very interesting year, you think as the boat pulls up to the dock in Venice.

"It's five o'clock already," says Duckie.

"How did it get so late?" you ask. "My mom is probably worried sick. I'd better get home."

"No, no," says Dario and several others. "Come to the castle. It will not be long."

If you stay with the group, turn to page 84.

If you go home, turn to page 87.

You reach up, and Russell takes a firm grip of your wrists.

"Climb up the wall of the rock as I pull," he tells you.

This is trust, you think as you place first one foot and then the other.

You are about halfway up when suddenly your foot slips and you start to slide. Russell tightens his grip. You are nearly dangling in the air. You struggle for a foothold. Finally, Russell pulls you over the top of the ledge. You are shaking. He takes you in his arms and holds you.

"You OK?" he asks softly.

"Yep," you say, breathing normally again. "In fact, I feel great!"

Above you, the mountain flattens out. Russell moves slower, and he turns around every minute to make sure you're behind him.

"Still here," you call, feeling pleased with your progress and proud that you didn't take the easy way out.

"Wow!" Russell yells as he reaches the top. "It's beautiful!" He takes your hand and helps you up the last ledge.

You stand there at the top of the mountain, awestruck. Down a craggy cliff is a secluded mountain lake bordered on one side by a dense forest and on the other side by a wide, open meadow. There are about fifteen deer drinking at the edge of the lake and grazing in the field.

(continued on page 75)

LOTS OF BOYS!

You turn to Russell. There are tears in your eyes.

"I can't believe this," you say. "Thank you for taking me here."

"What else could I ask for?" he says. "An incredible view and an incredible girl."

He puts his hands on your shoulders and pulls you close. Your heart is beating furiously, and there is a tingling in your whole body. He puts his arms around you and brings his lips to yours.

You are not only at the top of the mountain. You are at the top of the world.

The End

That's it! you think. *I don't know why I ever believed a word he said. How can he say those things to me and then . . .*

You can feel the tears coming to your eyes. *I'm such an idiot!*

You quickly find the door and let yourself out. By the time you reach the street there are tears streaming down your face.

No more Italians for me! you think as you run home.

The End

LOTS OF BOYS!

You look at your mother waiting for you in the doorway. You know that she will be disappointed, but you can hear the need in Russell's voice. You hope that she will understand.

"OK, Russ," you say. "Come over in a little while. I'll be here."

You explain to your mother that Russell has been having problems and that he sounded frightened when he called.

"I've been so worried about him, and this is the first time that he's asked for help. I just couldn't say no. I'm sorry."

Your mother looks hurt. "He's lucky to have a good friend like you," she says. And she gives you a hug and goes off in the car.

When Russell arrives, his eyes are red and his cheeks look swollen.

"Thanks," he says. "I really need to talk to someone."

What could be wrong? you think.

"I don't know how to begin," he says. "I . . . I . . . I took the money from work."

You say nothing. Russell's voice cracks; there are tears in his eyes.

"My father had a heart attack last week, and I had to get the money for a plane ticket. He lives in Washington, and he has no one."

Tears are streaming down his face. You put your arms around him.

"I'm sorry," you say.

(continued on page 78)

"I didn't know . . . I didn't know what to do. I didn't have the money to fly to Washington, and I couldn't get myself to ask anyone for it. So I . . . I . . ."

His voice breaks, and you hug him tightly. You have tears in your eyes as he continues.

"I'm flying out tomorrow afternoon. But I wanted you to know. And I want Maggie to know. I never thought that Denise would get blamed. I feel so stupid. I . . . I hate myself." He begins to sob.

You sit silently holding each other. You know that he is hurting so badly inside. You are touched that he trusts you, that he wanted to tell you his secret. You have never felt so close to anyone in your life.

"I can't face Maggie," he says. "But I want her to know. Will you tell her for me? Tell her I'll send her a check when I get the money. I promise."

You are uncomfortable with his request. Not because you are afraid to tell Maggie, but because something tells you that he should do it himself.

If you tell Maggie for him, turn to page 30.

If you tell him you cannot do that, turn to page 33.

"Burano," you say, giving them the name of the island you will visit first. Then you walk away.

"*Aspettate! Aspettate!*" the men yell.

"They are telling us to wait," Duckie says.

"No! *Arrivederci!*" she tells them. Good-bye.

You walk down the dock, climb onto the boat, and take a seat at the far end of the deck. You lean back, close your eyes, and relax.

"*Signorina!*" someone says, tapping you on the shoulder. You open your eyes and see one of the men from the dock. The other two men are standing next to him.

"*Ciao, belle ragazze!*" one says.

"Oh, brother!" says Duckie. "Come on!"

She takes your arm and pulls you to the other side of the boat. The men follow.

"*Volete ballare sta sera?*" Do you want to go dancing tonight? another man says.

"No!" you say. "Go away!"

The men follow you off the boat. You try to enjoy the scenery, but you keep hearing "*ragazze, belle ragazze*" behind you.

For the rest of the day, through all the islands, the men follow. Your whole day is ruined.

Next time, you vow, *I will keep my plans to myself.*

The End

As you round the corner, you spot Marzio standing in front of his canvas, facing the water. You walk slowly toward him, a bit nervous, but confident that he will be happy to see you.

You come up behind him and put your hand on his shoulder.

"Hello!" you say.

He turns around. *"Ciao,"* he says. "How nice to see you again."

That's an odd way of greeting me after last night, you think.

"You have been well?" he says.

"Fine," you say, but you wonder if something is wrong. His tone of voice is distant.

Besides, you think, *what a dumb question. How much could have happened to me since last night?*

You suddenly feel very uncomfortable. Marzio is not reacting the way you expected. In fact, he has gone back to his painting!

"Um, I . . . I just wanted to tell you that my mother said it was fine to go to your party," you say.

"My party?" he says, looking at you strangely.

"Yes," you say. "You invited me to the surprise party for your brother." *How could he have forgotten?* you wonder, both angry and hurt.

"Mamma mia," he shouts and hits his head and shakes his arm. "You think I am Marzio?"

"Of course I think you are Marzio. That's because you are Marzio."

What is going on? you think. *Is he crazy?*

(continued on page 81)

"No, no, no, no, no. Now I understand. I am not Marzio. I am Marco. Marzio is my brother. We are twins."

You look at him in disbelief.

"Now, you talked about a party. A party for me. My brother is having a party for me?"

Oh, no, you think. *I have ruined the surprise.*

You cannot believe this has happened! You want to crawl into a hole and hide. You have just ruined Marzio's surprise while at the same time making a fool of yourself.

Sometimes there's just no way of predicting how things will turn out.

The End

Russell puts the glass down, and you fill it up with water.

She deserves it, you think, as you place the glass on the table.

"Is there anything else I can get you?" you say in a sweet voice.

"Not right now," she says.

As you stand there, the woman takes a sip of water. She dribbles down the front of her sweater. Fighting back laughter, you walk quickly to the back of the restaurant to join Russell in the viewing box.

She drinks again. More dribbles. This time she takes a napkin and wipes herself off.

"Waitress," she calls. "Another napkin please." You bring one over.

She takes another sip, and once again the water dribbles down her front. You and Russell are laughing so hysterically, you have to run into the kitchen. When you come back out, the woman has gotten up and is walking toward the ladies' room. Suddenly she stops and picks up something from the serving counter. You lean over to see what she has and discover that she is holding the dribble glass carton in her hand.

"Uh oh," you say, knowing that you should be feeling scared, but unable to keep yourself from laughing.

(continued on page 83)

LOTS OF BOYS!

"What kind of a place is this?" she yells, furiously. "How dare you treat me like this! I wouldn't give you a dime!" She storms out the door and slams it shut.

You and Russell are rolling on the floor laughing. When you finally regain your composure, you each reach in your pocket and take out three dollars . . . to cover the unpaid check.

It was worth every penny!

The End

You look at Dario. "You will not be sorry to come," he says. "We will entertain you." He begins to do an Irish jig.

How can I refuse such an absolute nut? you think. "All right, I'll go to the castle with you."

Dario picks you up and spins you around. "I am glad you stay," he says.

As the boat speeds across the water, you lean your head back and let the wind blow through your hair. You feel such a wonderful sense of freedom and independence.

The boat docks at the foot of a huge castle, and you all pile out. You, Dario, and Duckie hold hands and sing Beatles songs as you walk up the stairs. Dario knows all the words in English.

Between exploring the castle and taking pictures, the time flies by. Before you realize it, the sun is setting. As the boat heads back to Venice, the sky is a blazing orange. The scene is absolutely breathtaking.

"You will come to my work—to my *gelateria*—tonight?" Dario says. "I will make you the best ice cream in Italy."

"Yes," you say. "Duckie and I will be there."

Dario quacks and smiles. You thank everyone over and over again. Then you and Duckie walk toward your houses.

"Can you believe it?" Duckie says. "Aren't they the neatest people?"

You fly home and take the stairs two at a time.

(continued on page 85)

"Mom," you shout, "I'm home."

Your mother walks slowly into the living room where you have collapsed on the couch. You take one look at her expression and sit up straight.

"Young lady, do you realize what time it is? I have been worried sick. I thought something had happened to you. I give you independence, and you abuse it. Well, my dear, that's it. From now on, you'd better work on some responsibility."

You don't move. You know there is no point in asking her about going out tonight.

The End

The girl says a few words to the woman and walks toward the door. Your head says, *Try. Just go over and ask if she can help you.* Your heart pounds. But your feet don't move.

The woman behind the counter smiles at you and shrugs her shoulders. You are frustrated and embarrassed. You can feel the tears building in your eyes. You run out the door.

I'll never go in there again, you think as you race home, up the stairs, and onto your bed. You are furious with yourself. You ran away from the painter. You ran out of the store. You couldn't even talk to someone your own age!

If I keep this up, you think, *I'll spend this whole year talking to my mother!*

The End

"Thanks a lot," you say. "But I really have to go home."

"*Ma bambolina*. How can you leave?" Dario says, taking your hand. "You promise to come to my work?"

"OK," you say. "We'll come." You hit Duckie. "Won't we?"

"Oh, sure, yes, your work," she says.

You and Duckie wave good-bye and walk toward your house. You are a block away when you glance back at the boat. Dario is still waving to you. When he sees you looking, he begins to jump up and down and wave both hands.

"What does *bambolina* mean?" you ask Duckie.

"I think it means little doll," she says.

You burst out laughing.

"What a nut!" you say.

"You're not kidding!" she agrees.

You and Duckie make plans to meet a few days later.

"Maybe we'll go see Dario," you say.

You spend the next days getting settled. By the end of the week, you are dying to see Duckie and do something.

"I'll be home by ten," you tell your mom as you go out the door.

You run all the way to Duckie's, and the two of you head for Caffè Roma.

"You go first!" you say, pushing Duckie ahead of you.

(continued on page 88)

"No way, this was your idea," she says.

You reach for the door, and it flies open.

"Ciao! Ciao!" Dario yells. He is wearing a bright blue baseball hat with horns. *"Bambolina!"*

He picks you up and spins you around. He seats you at a table and runs back to the counter, singing and dancing as he works.

For the next week you and Duckie return to Caffè Roma every night. One night you even bring your mother. As soon as Dario sees her, he rushes out the door and comes back with a flower for her. That was the night he was wearing Mickey Mouse ears. The next night he was wearing clown shoes in two different colors.

Every time you come in, Dario makes you ice cream surprises.

"We are going to get fat," you say.

"Even then you will be beautiful," he tells you.

By the end of two weeks, you and Dario have become very good friends . . . not romantic friends, but good, and funny friends. You love being with him; he makes you laugh. And he loves to have you around. You know that he will be an important part of your year in Italy.

One Friday night, you and Duckie arrive at Caffè Roma at eight o'clock. The tables are all taken and there is a line at the counter. Dario is wearing a beanie with a propeller on top.

"Ciao, bambolina!" he yells, waving both arms.

(continued on page 89)

LOTS OF BOYS! 89

You wave back. Suddenly, someone taps Duckie on the shoulder. "Susan?" says a tall, blond American.

"Scusa?" says Duckie in Italian.

"Oh, I'm sorry," says the boy. "I—thought—you—were—somebody—else," he says slowly. He hits another American who is standing next to him. "I think these girls are Italian," you hear him say. "If they are, they're the first Italian girls we've met." He turns back to you and Duckie. "Where—are—you—from?"

If you say you are from Italy, turn to page 35.

If you tell them you're American, turn to page 54.

Maybe another time, you think. *I hardly even know her. Besides, she might not even think it's funny.*

You wander through the streets. Patrizia points out her favorite clothing stores and caffès and bakeries. You arrive at the dock right on time. Masimo is anxiously waiting.

As you walk toward him, Patrizia whispers, "I think my brother likes you. He wishes very much he spoke English."

"Ciao!" Massimo says with a big smile. He stares at you, eyes wide open. Then he motions for you to come into the boat. You and Patrizia climb into the lavish gondola and onto a cushioned seat. Massimo follows. He takes his long oar and steers the boat into a narrow canal. He says something in Italian to Patrizia.

"He says we have an hour before the . . . the . . . fireworks," Patrizia tells you. "He will take us for a ride."

As Massimo paddles, he stares straight at the back of your head. Every time you turn around, he has a dumb, dazed expression on his face.

Why won't he stop? you wonder, as he stares at you with a drippy smile. *This is ridiculous.*

Soon, Massimo begins to sing a song from an Italian opera. You feel compelled to look at him as he sings.

You plant a smile on your face and turn to watch him. He is paddling through a narrow canal, staring

(continued on page 91)

straight at you and singing words that must be about love. You could die! He is paying no attention whatsoever to where he is or what he is doing. He is just staring into your eyes and singing.

Suddenly, Patrizia screams, "Massimo, *sta attento!*"

But she is too late! The boat crashes into a dock. You are jolted sideways. Patrizia crashes into you; and Massimo follows. The boat tilts, and you all tumble into the filthy, mucky water.

You have heard stories about the dirty water in the Venice canals, but you did not expect to find out this way!

The End

You try not to look at him. You look down at the ground; you follow the flight of a pigeon; you pretend to be interested in a little American girl who is walking by with her parents. The painter is walking straight toward you. You cannot avoid him any longer.

"Ciao, bella!" the tall, dark-haired guy says to you. You look at him and smile nervously.

"Hello," you say, noticing his deep, chocolate brown eyes and his dimples. *He is gorgeous,* you think, trying to act very nonchalant.

"Ah, Americana?" he says.

You nod.

"I would like to ask of you something," he says, struggling with the English. "I like to paint a beautiful girl as you." He hesitates. "Your hair is like gold in the sun."

I can't believe he just said that, you think.

"If you stay sitting, I can then paint your beauty."

By now, you are ready to die. *This guy is straight out of a movie,* you think. *I sure know I'm in a foreign country; at home a guy would jump in front of a moving truck before he would tell a girl she's beautiful!* It feels weird, but it feels terrific, too.

"I guess I could sit here for a while," you say.

His face lights up.

"Ah, sei dolce! Bellisima!" he says as he kisses your hand. You have no idea what he just said, but it sounded nice.

He introduces himself, but you don't understand

(continued on page 93)

LOTS OF BOYS!

his name. *I'll think of him as George,* you decide. You're not sure how it began, but whenever you and your friends at home see a cute boy you call him George. And this boy is definitely cute. You introduce yourself.

George then brings his easel over and begins painting. Every few minutes he just stares at you.

"Bella. Bella. Beautiful," he keeps saying.

You don't know quite what to do, so you just sit there with a half smile on your face, looking into his wonderful eyes as he stares intently at you and then at his canvas.

Finally, he motions for you to come and look at the painting. The portrait is incredible; it is soft and gentle. It looks very much like you, yet there is depth and mystery to the girl on the canvas.

The painter takes your hand and kisses it. "Thank you," he says. "Thank you very much. Please come to see me again."

You race home along the streets and alleys and arrive with about a half an hour to get ready before Mr. Bandonelli is due to pick you up for dinner at his house. You shower and throw on clothes.

I don't have to fuss for dinner with a group of adults, you think, deciding not to bother with makeup.

As you walk to his house, Mr. Bandonelli tells you some of the history of Venice. You cannot concentrate on what he is telling you; you can only think about the painter.

(continued on page 94)

When you walk in the door, you are greeted by Mrs. Bandonelli, a heavyset woman with open arms and a warm smile. She hugs you, kisses you on each cheek, and leads you into a small living room filled with exquisite antiques and paintings of Venice.

You pivot around the room to get a full view, and your eyes stop suddenly. There, among the canvases leaning against the wall, is your portrait!

It can't be, you think. You walk closer. *But it is!*

"I see you are interested in the paintings," says Mr. Bandonelli. "My son paints all of these."

Your knees feel weak. You cannot believe that you are going to have dinner with George. Then Mrs. Bandonelli calls everyone to dinner. You wish you had put make-up on. You never dreamed that it would matter! After all, you were having dinner with your mother and her boss!

You sit down at the table, and Mrs. Bandonelli serves the first course. The table, you discover, is set for four. You wonder where he could be, who he is with. You laugh at yourself because you are feeling jealous.

The meal is incredible! Homemade spaghetti with a bacon, egg, and cheese sauce is piled on your plate. You are full before you are halfway finished, but you struggle to get it down. Then three big pieces of chicken are placed in front of you. You cannot finish them.

"Non ti piace? You don't like?" says Mrs. Bandonelli.

(continued on page 95)

"No, I love it! But I have a small appetite," you say.

Then come salad, salami, and cheeses and cake. By the time the fruit arrives you are sure that you will have to be rolled home.

"Oh, I almost forgot!" Mr. Bandonelli says, throwing his hands in the air. He directs his conversation to you. "My son, Marzio, would like to take you to see Venice tomorrow evening. He could not be here tonight, but he asked me to say this to you. Would you like to go?"

Is he kidding? you think. *Hmm. Marzio, so that's his name! What a beautiful name. Marzio! Much better than George.*

"Absolutely," you say, fighting back the urge to cartwheel across the room.

"Good," says Mr. Bandonelli. "He will pick you up at your house at 6:30."

This is not a choice. This is an opportunity. Turn to page 66.

"Russell, I just can't!" you say. "I promised my mother . . ."

"Don't worry about it," he says and hangs up.

But you do. You worry about him all night long: you barely see the show, and you eat nothing.

The next morning Russell never shows up for work. You call his apartment, and no one answers. Later, you tell Chuck about the phone call.

"You're kidding?" he says. "Russ called me too, but I was on my way out the door. I told him I'd call later. . . . I guess I forgot."

You and Chuck take turns calling Russell's apartment every half-hour for the rest of the day. At seven o'clock, Russell's roommate answers the phone.

"I've been wondering about the same thing," he tells you when you ask him where Russell is. "I just got home, and all his clothes are gone."

After work, you and Chuck try to figure out where he might have gone. That's when you realize how little you both know about Russell. You know nothing about his family or even where they live. You only know about the Russell who lives and works and goes to school in Crystal, Colorado. And you both know that you have grown to love him very much. The other thing you know is that neither of you was there when he needed you.

Two weeks pass. You and Chuck have been totally depressed. Maggie has fired Denise on the pretext that she showed up late three times in one

(continued on page 97)

LOTS OF BOYS!

week. But you and Chuck know that Denise was fired on circumstantial evidence. Maggie was convinced that Denise took the money, even though nothing was ever proven. Russell would have been furious!

Most of the fun has gone out of work . . . and play has practically ended. You and Chuck do things together, but the craziness seems to have ended when Russell disappeared.

Two weeks go by and you still have not heard a word. Then one day a letter arrives. There is a check enclosed made out to Maggie for $150.

> I don't know how to say this, except I'm sorry. I know you guys are probably concerned about me, but I had a lot to work out in my head.
>
> Yes, I stole the money. I had found out a few days earlier that my father had had a heart attack and was on the critical list. I couldn't afford the plane fare, and I just had to get here. I always intended to return the money.
>
> I didn't like leaving without talking to you. But I tried, and you were both busy.
>
> I am now with my father, and he is recovering. I doubt that I'll be coming back to Crystal . . . partly because my family needs me, and partly because I feel strange about having taken off the way I did.
>
> Please tell Maggie I'm sorry. I hope Denise wasn't made to pay for my crime, but I tried to defend her. It's interesting how much you learn about appearance and reality when something like this happens.
>
> Take care.
>
> Love,
> Russell

(continued on page 98)

There is no phone number . . . and no return address.

Neither you nor Chuck will ever know if things might have turned out differently if you had been there for Russell when he wanted to talk. What you do know is that you will always, from now on, be available to your friends when they need you.

The End

LOTS OF BOYS! 99

You can barely move. You just sit there, speechless.

I can't wait for an explanation, you think. *Boy is he going to hear from me!*

You sit there stewing. *He wishes he could only be with me!* you remember him saying. *Right! Me and the lady in the black dress!*

You see Marzio walking toward you. Someone is walking behind him. All you can see is another gray suit.

That must be his brother, you think.

As Marzio approaches you, you can feel your whole body tighten.

"*Bella!*" he says as he reaches for your hand.

You snap your hand away.

"Don't call me *bella!*" you say.

"I do not understand," he says, looking confused.

"I saw you over . . ." You stop. Walking up behind him is a guy who looks exactly like Marzio.

"Ah," says the guy, "the beautiful American in my painting."

"The painter!" you yell. "But I thought . . ." You burst into laughter. *They are twins!* you realize. *I don't believe it!*

(continued on page 100)

"You thought I was kissing . . ." Marzio starts to laugh. His brother joins him.

When you finally calm down, Marzio takes your hand.

"Excuse me, Marco," he says and leads you into another room.

"You are the only one I will kiss!" he says, and he presses his lips to yours.

When you open your eyes, you are looking into his. They are sparkling.

And you are the only one I will kiss, you think.

The End

LOTS OF BOYS! 101

The girl takes her groceries and walks toward the door. You take a deep breath and tap her on the shoulder.

"Excuse me," you say. "Do you speak English?"

She smiles. "Yes, a little."

You smile back and explain your problem. She says a few words to the owner, and you are handed a container of orange juice.

"That was so simple," you say. "It is so frustrating not being able to speak Italian."

"I know what that feels like," she says as you walk out the door together. "When I went to England to learn English, I did not know any. Now I do not speak well, still."

"You speak English wonderfully," you say. "If I could only speak Italian that well."

"I know!" she says. "I teach to you Italian if you give help to me in my English."

"It's a deal," you say.

"I am Patrizia," she says. You introduce yourself.

Patrizia tells you that she will be away for two weeks. She will call you when she returns.

You give her your address and telephone number and you both take off in opposite directions.

You smile all the way home. *I met an Italian!* you say to yourself. *I'm going to learn to speak!* You race up the stairs.

For the next couple of weeks you are very busy. You wander in and out of the streets and alleys, mentally noting everything you see. You listen to

(continued on page 102)

people talking and try to understand what they are saying. You watch the way people talk with their hands; and you are intrigued by the exuberance of the Italians.

Every day around four o'clock, you end up at a little caffè near San Marco. You went in there one day for a soda, and you were surrounded by four handsome waiters about your age. They loved practicing their English with you, and they asked you to come back.

After your second visit, they stopped charging you for your drinks, and then they started to bring you a different pastry every day . . . all on the house. You are especially proud of the fact that you have met them on your own.

You love the attention when they gather around you and talk, but you are very frustrated when they speak among themselves in Italian . . . especially when you know they are talking and laughing about you. They look at you and talk animatedly, with their hands punctuating their speech. You can't stand not knowing what they are saying.

Toward the end of the two weeks, you are eagerly anticipating Patrizia's call. One day you decide to stay home and do some cleaning and the last of the unpacking. You have been working all day, moving boxes, scrubbing the bathroom, ironing clothes. Your hair is filthy, so you have tied it up in a bandana; and you can actually smell your sweaty body. As a final act, before you take a bath, you dust the

(continued on page 103)

LOTS OF BOYS! 103

window sill. Outside, there are two children playing ball. You are watching them when you notice a girl and a guy in front of the building next door.

It's Patrizia! you realize. She is walking up and down your street followed by a short guy with curly brown hair. *What is she doing?* you think.

You open the window to yell, and then you remember what you look like. You see her stare up at your building and then walk on.

If you call out to greet her, turn to page 40.

If you don't want to be seen like this, turn to page 44.

You are holding your shoes when Marzio jogs back to you and grabs your hand.

"Let's go," he says, and you both run toward the first gondola in line. He helps you into the long, black boat. The gondolier follows Marzio in.

You and Marzio sit, side by side, on a large, cushioned seat in the back of the boat. The man stands in the front and pushes off with a long oar.

As you move—first along busy canals and later through dark, secluded ones—you feel as though you are in a movie. Marzio puts his arm around you, and you snuggle into his warm, receptive body. The gondolier begins singing a slow, romantic song in Italian. You close your eyes and dream.

When the boat pulls over, Marzio helps you out. You look up and realize that you are right in front of your house.

"What service!" you say, smiling.

"Anything for you, my little pepper," Marzio says. He walks you to your door and turns you toward him. Holding both of your hands, he kisses you gently on each cheek.

"I would like to see you again," he says. "I must work tomorrow, but I am having a surprise party for my brother in two days. You will come? It is for his graduation."

"I would like that, but I must ask my mother first," you say.

"Of course," he says. "I am sure she will say yes. But you must keep the party a big secret. My

(continued on page 105)

LOTS OF BOYS! 105

brother must not find out. I have been planning it for a month now, and there are only two days more. If he finds out, it will ruin everything! I am very happy for tonight. I will call you tomorrow."

Once again, he kisses you on each cheek. Then he walks down the stairs.

You walk into your house and collapse onto the couch, happier than you have ever been in your life.

The next morning, you tell your mother all about your evening. When you finish, she has tears in her eyes.

"Oh, Mother!" you say.

"But that is so romantic," she says. "I wish I were your age again."

While you eat your breakfast of a roll and jam, you think of Marzio. While you get dressed, you think of Marzio. In fact, you cannot think of anything else. As you are walking toward Plaza San Marco, you have a sudden urge to see him.

He said he was working today, you think. *And I know where he works.*

If you choose to surprise Marzio at the dock where he paints, turn to page 80.

If you wait for his call instead, turn to page 106.

Every time the phone rings, you jump. You make your mother answer it all day.

I don't want to seem anxious, you decide.

Finally, at six o'clock the phone rings.

"Just a moment, please," you hear your mother say.

"Hello?" you say.

"Ciao, dolce," Marzio says. "I am missing you."

Just hearing his voice makes your body tingle. You explain that you will come to the party, but that first you must have dinner with your mother and some of her friends. You will arrive late.

"This is OK," he says. "I just want to see you. I will count the hours."

You have no idea how to respond to that, so you ask him what you should wear.

"Ah," he says. "I know you will look beautiful in anything, but I think the women will be wearing dresses. I will wear a suit."

It seems like forever until tomorrow night. You, too, are counting the hours.

Finally, the time arrives. You finish dinner and you rush over to the Bandonelli house. Marzio answers the door. He is wearing a dark gray suit and a white shirt, and he looks like a movie star.

"My beautiful *Americana!*" he says, hugging you. "I have missed you . . . your smile, your hair, your eyes!"

You are enchanted.

When you pull your eyes away from him, you

(continued on page 107)

LOTS OF BOYS!

discover a crowded room filled with mostly men wearing dark suits. Except for their faces, they are all lean, dark, and good-looking. Marzio, of course, is the best-looking of all.

"I wish to be only with you tonight," Marzio says.

Me too, you think.

"But I must see that everyone is happy. If I leave your side, you must understand. Now, what would you like to drink?"

He takes your hand and walks you into the kitchen. You ask for a Coke.

"And now," he says, staring into your eyes, "you must have something to eat."

He leads you to the dining room table filled with wonderful things: shrimp and salads and chicken and red peppers and salami and cheeses and breads.

"I just came from dinner," you say.

"Ah, yes, I forget," he says.

The doorbell rings.

"I will be back," he says, walking toward the door.

You feel as though you are floating on a cloud . . . *or maybe a gondola,* you think.

You look around the room. There are small groups of people, all speaking Italian and gesturing with their hands. You look from group to group, wondering what they are talking about and if you will ever learn their beautiful language.

I'm so lucky to be here, you think as you look

(continued on page 108)

around for Marzio. You see him in the dining room. He is talking to a tall, beautiful brunette. She is wearing a slinky black dress.

You feel your stomach tighten.

He has to greet the guests, you tell yourself.

He keeps moving closer and closer to her as they speak. You don't want to watch, but you can't stop. He takes her hand and they walk into another room.

How dare he! you think. Then you stop yourself. *Maybe they're just good friends.*

A moment later Marzio comes over to you with a pastry. Once more, he looks into your eyes and tells you how beautiful you are.

She must be a friend, you think as you take a bite of the pastry.

"You like?" he says.

"Yes, it is very sweet," you say.

"Sweet, like you," he says, taking your hand.

Definitely a friend! you decide.

"I would like you to meet my brother," he says. "I will go find him."

Again, Marzio leaves. You sit down and scan the room. Suddenly, you see Marzio. He is standing in a corner, kissing the girl in the black dress. You can feel your body burning.

That is no friend!!

If you get up and leave, turn to page 76.

If you stay, turn to page 99.

LOTS OF BOYS!

The next day, as you walk out of the kitchen balancing a salad, a quiche, and a bowl of soup, you see Russell hand Greg his camera.

Oh, well, you think. *There goes a romance that never got off the ground.*

You follow Greg with your eyes as he walks out the door. Unfortunately, eyes cannot be in two places at once; you crash into a customer who is on her way to the ladies' room. The soup, cold gazpacho, plops out of the bowl and all over you, the floor, and the customer; and the quiche slides off the plate.

"Ladies and gentlemen," Russell calls. "For her next act, Lola will make spaghetti fly across the room."

You stick your tongue out at him, since you have no extra hands to hit him.

All afternoon you and Russell are alone. Every time you walk into the kitchen, he takes your arms and leads you in the tango, cheek-to-cheek.

On one trip, he presents you with a dead carnation from an old flower arrangement. "A flower for you, my darling."

"Why thank you, my dear!" you say with a curtsey. *What a nut,* you think.

For the next few weeks, you, Russell, and Chuck are constantly together. Russell is always coming up with some crazy idea, and he easily cons you and Chuck into going along. At first you try to include Denise, but she always says no. She doesn't even

(continued on page 110)

talk to you at work. You all agree that she's a little weird.

One slow afternoon Chuck marches out of the kitchen. "Odd Squad meeting!" he calls. "There's an important matter to discuss." He takes your hand and pulls you into the kitchen. Russell marches behind you.

"Well, now," says Chuck, clearing his throat. "Tomorrow is Monday. That means another day off. Last week we three went water-skiing. The week before we went sailing. What will it be this week?"

"I would like to suggest a wonderful new activity," says Russell, "an ancient game that I used to play with my father called—rewind baseball."

"What?" you ask.

"Ah, you don't know the game? Let me briefly explain. It is like baseball, only you run the bases backwards . . . that is, you run to third base, first; second base, second; and first base, third. Oh, and you also run backwards. And every time you come to a base, you run in a backward circle around the base."

"Sounds real simple," says Chuck. "I say we go all out for rewind baseball."

"A wonderful opportunity to learn a truly classic game," you say. "You guys are nuts!"

After the ball game the next day you go for ice cream and then a movie. You walk to the theatre between the boys, each one holding one of your hands.

(continued on page 111)

LOTS OF BOYS! 111

What would I do without them? you think.

Chuck goes up to get the tickets for all of you, leaving you and Russell standing there holding hands. Suddenly a strange thing happens. Russell squeezes your hand slightly and you feel a chill run up your arm and through your body. You turn to look at him and his deep blue eyes penetrate into yours. Your eyes lock.

What is happening? you think, as you suddenly become aware of your messy hair and your dirty shirt. You have never felt this way with Russell before.

"We're all set," Chuck announces when he returns. He takes your hand and leads you into the theatre. Within a few seconds everything is back to normal.

"I'll go get popcorn," Russell says. "You guys get seats. Hold up a flag so I can find you."

The next day you work with Chuck. It's a quiet day, and you end up telling family stories all day long. Denise just sits by the register, alone.

"Why doesn't she talk to us?" you ask Chuck.

"You mean you don't know? No one has ever told you that you smell?"

You hit him over the head.

During the day you find yourself asking Chuck questions about Russell's background. You discover that he doesn't know any more than you do about where he's from or what his family is like.

(continued on page 112)

"Beneath that outgoing exterior," says Chuck, "he's a very private person."

"Hey," Maggie calls from the kitchen. "It's after five. Where's the third musketeer?"

"He'll be here soon," you say, looking forward to Russell's arrival.

"Not soon," he says, flying through the door. "I have arrived. He pretends to be holding a sword. Chuck joins in, and they have a duel.

"It's over you," Chuck says to you. "And one of us must die."

"No! No!" you say, mimicking a heroine. "Stop! Stop!"

"Oh, you kids!" Maggie says, shaking her head. "I have some paychecks, if you can return to the world for a minute." The three of you race over.

The rest of the week drags on. You are so sick of looking at salads and soups that you are thinking of opening a junk food stand—only foods that will rot teeth or fill arteries with cholesterol.

Finally Sunday arrives. Only one more day until your day off. You wonder what new madness is in store, and you can't wait for Russell to get to work so you can make plans for the Odd Squad's outing of the week. Chuck is off for the day, and you have been looking forward to being alone with Russell. The two of you always have so much fun.

You and Russell are overwhelmed by the brunch crowd. It seems as though every family in town has decided to have brunch at your restaurant. There

(continued on page 113)

are screaming babies, hyperactive six-year-olds, and harried parents. But the worst customer of the morning is a demanding woman in her fifties. She keeps calling you over and complaining.

"Young lady, this spoon is dirty"; "These eggs are too soft!"; "This corn muffin is crumbly. Bring me a blueberry."

Didn't anyone ever teach you the word "please"? you think.

When you are busy, she calls Russell over and complains to him. You are both ready to kill her. You also suspect that she has planned to spend her Sunday in your restaurant. She arrived at ten and, two hours later when nearly everyone else has left, she is still making demands.

Finally, she is the only one left, and you join Russell at the back of the restaurant.

"Ah," he says. "Just the person I've been waiting for. I want you to taste my specialty drink."

He hands you a glass of liquid. It looks like club soda. It smells like club soda. You take a sip. It tastes like club soda. You are very glad it is like club soda because, in sipping it, you dribble down the front of your blouse.

"It's club soda," you say, grabbing a napkin and wiping yourself.

"Wrong," says Russell. "Drink some more."

"You are so weird!" you say, and you take a big gulp, spilling some more down the front of your blouse.

(continued on page 114)

Russell is hysterical. "Slob," he says, laughing.

"This *is* club soda!" you scream.

"Right," says Russell, and he holds up a carton that says "Dribble Glass."

"You idiot," you say, laughing. "What am I going to do with you?"

"Waitress! Waiter!" yells the woman. "Can I have some water? What kind of service do you call this?"

You look at Russell.

If you give the woman her water in Russell's glass, turn to page 82.

If you don't, turn to page 24.

LOTS OF BOYS!

Patrizia cannot stop laughing when you tell her your idea.

"I like this," she says. "But they will know I am Italian."

"Let's just try. They'll think you're American if you're with me. Just don't talk."

"I am American," she says, winking at you.

As you walk in the door, two of the waiters come rushing over.

"Ciao, bella," says Enzo, a light brown-haired boy with a sparkling white smile.

"Ciao!" echoes a taller, dark-haired boy with a turned-up nose and dark brown eyes. He puts his arm around you. "Today you bring a friend?"

"Ciao," you say. "This is my friend, Patty. Patty, this is Enzo and Giampiero." Your other two friends suddenly emerge from inside. "And Franco and Bepe."

"It is very nice to meet you," Patrizia says.

You look for a reaction from the guys, but there is none.

"I haven't seen you in a while," you say. "I've been busy."

Giampiero says something in Italian, and the other guys laugh. To you he says, "It has been a few days. We miss you."

Patrizia leans over close to you and says quietly, "He just said that he does not miss you because he sees you in his dreams all the time."

You know that your face is turning red.

(continued on page 116)

"You would like to stand here at bar or maybe sit?" Giampiero asks. Then he leans toward Enzo and speaks in Italian. Again, they laugh.

Patrizia translates: "I wish they would stand. When they are standing, I can better see their beautiful bodies."

"We will sit!" you say emphatically, plopping down in a chair.

The boys run off to get you drinks; they are jabbering in Italian among themselves. Patrizia listens.

"Enzo said that all Americans girls are beautiful," Patrizia tells you.

"They really think you're American, Patty," you say.

"This makes me very happy," she says. "I am American from California." She laughs.

When Giampiero and Enzo bring over two Cokes, they are arguing. Patrizia nudges you.

"They want to ask of us to go to a party tomorrow," she says. "They fight for who asks."

She stops talking and smiles as the boys walk over. You have to hold your breath to keep from laughing.

"I . . ." Enzo begins. "I . . ."

"We would love to go to your party," Patrizia says in Italian, smiling.

The two boys stop short.

"Come?" Enzo says. *"Parli Italiano?"*

Patrizia tells them in Italian what she has been doing.

(continued on page 117)

LOTS OF BOYS!

"Mamma mia!" Stefano yells, babbling in Italian.

"They are very embarrassed for what they said before," Patrizia says, and you all start to laugh.

"You are very *furba*. How you say in English?" he says to Patrizia.

"Sneaky," she says.

"Yes. Sneaky. You will come to the party next week? Yes?" he says.

"Yes. I will be happy to come to the party," you say.

Suddenly you realize that an hour has passed and you are due at the dock. You and Patrizia agree to come by the caffè tomorrow. You both rush out into the street.

"Ciao, Patty!" yells one of the boys.

You all laugh.

The End